## Contents

/*
# INTRODUCTION: GERALD MCLAVERTY
*/

People become homeless for a variety of reasons, some by choice and others by accident or bad luck. Anyone can potentially become a homeless person. After spending several years on the street experiencing homelessness first hand, I have developed strong views on the subject. I believe that one of the most important things is to keep things as brief and simple as possible to avoid confusion. People can become ill, end up in prison, or even end up dead as a result of homelessness. I believe fighting homelessness is an ongoing battle that needs to be managed in the best possible way. There are many charities that claim to help the homeless, and a lot of the money made by these organizations often doesn't make it to street level and is unnecessarily wasted on things like administration and overheads.

I designed this simple list of questions written from a homeless person's point of view. What do I need and what do I expect to find? I believe there are many places in the United Kingdom that do not have adequate answers to these questions and I am trying to raise awareness in order to improve the situation for people in the future. It may even save lives.

Gerald Mclaverty

# /* Frequently Asked Questions */

Anthony Luvera
Gerald Mclaverty

Where can I find shelter when it is raining or snowing?

Where can I get a bath or shower?

Where can I go to a toilet during the night?

Where can I go to a toilet during the day?

Where can I get clothes, footwear and a blanket?

Where can I wash my clothes?

Where can I sleep during the night that is safe?

Where can I go to use a telephone?

Where can I go to see a doctor?

Where can I go to use a computer?

Where can I go to see a dentist?

Where can I access facilities for my pet dog (food, bags for waste, vetcare)?

# /* INTRODUCTION: ANTHONY LUVERA */

If you were homeless, where would you go for help? Frequently Asked Questions uncovers the shocking and poignant challenge faced by those asking this one simple question.

The research behind Frequently Asked Questions began in 2014 as part of Assembly, a larger body of work made with over 50 homeless people living in Brighton and Hove, commissioned by Brighton Photo Fringe. Seeking a way to present research about support and services available to people experiencing homelessness, I struck up a collaboration with Gerald Mclaverty. This involved sending email correspondence to council representatives in cities and towns across the UK, written from Gerald's experience of homelessness, requesting information about services provided in each locality.

At the heart of Frequently Asked Questions are several questions that ask about a homeless individual's right to access to basic living provisions such as shelter, personal safety, health, food, and communication. It is Gerald's firm belief that councils around the UK do not always have adequate answers to these questions.

Throughout 2017, Gerald and I undertook further research with a new round of enquiries which was exhibited as part of State of the Nation with Museum of Homelessness at Tate Liverpool in January 2018. Considering the introduction of the Homelessness Reduction Act 2017, which legally bound local authorities with new duties in relation to homeless individuals, we thought it was an important moment to conduct further questioning of councils in 2019 to see if the Act had resulted in any discernible change in their behaviour, in effect putting their performance under the microscope. Further exhibitions were held at The People's Republic of Stokes Croft in Bristol from November to December 2019, and at The Gallery at Foyles in London from January to February 2020.

Frequently Asked Questions is more than a display of data at an exhibition or in a publication. It is an invitation to take part in a conversation. Space is made to ask the audience, 'What Are Your Questions?' to enable viewers to directly contribute to future research by providing responses and suggestions that can be folded into the life of the project, bringing to the fore more questions that need to be asked. Audiences actively contribute to activities ranging from public discussions, workshops, reflective spaces, and creative responses. These events are staged in collaboration with artists, activists, campaigners, organisations and experts working across disciplines to shake up preconceptions, lobby for change, and prompt people to think differently, such as IC Visual Lab, The Bristol Cable, Liverpool Salon, and the Museum of Homelessness's Dying Homeless Project.

I invite you to contemplate this information and the range of responses provided by local authorities. It depicts how services both help and hinder people, and gives insight into the challenges faced by the most marginalised individuals in society as they attempt to access systems of care.

Anthony Luvera

# /* THE CONTEXT */

**Housing (Homeless Persons) Act 1977**
The Housing (Homeless Persons) Act (1977) made local authorities responsible for the long-term rehousing of some groups of homeless people for the first time. The Act defined which groups of homeless people were considered to have a 'priority need' and therefore might be owed a duty to be secured accommodation by local authorities.

**Homelessness Reduction Act 2017**
The Homelessness Reduction Act became law in April 2017 following extensive campaigning from Crisis and affiliated groups. The law places new duties on councils to aid those who are or may become homeless, regardless of priority need categories. This was the first major piece of homelessness legislation to be enacted into law in the UK for 15 years. It came into force in April 2018.

/*
THE
ENQUIRY
*/

# Frequently Asked Questions

**To** Aberdeen Council; Antrim & Newtonabbey Council; Ards Council; Armagh Council; Bangor Council; Barking & Dagenham Council; Barnet Council; Belfast Council; Bexley Council; Birmingham Council; Blackpool Council; Bournemouth Council; Bradford Council; Brent Council; Brighton Council; Bristol Council; Bromley Council; Caerphilly Council; Cambridge Council; Camden Council; Canterbury Council; Cardiff Council; Carlisle Council; Chelmsford Council; City of London Council; Connah's Quay Council; Coventry Council; Croydon Council; Derby Council; Derry Strabane Council; Dundee Council; Durham Council; Ealing Council; Edinburgh Council; Enfield Council; Exeter Council; Fife Council; Glasgow Council; Gloucester Council; Greenwich Council; Hackney Council; Hammersmith & Fulham Council; Haringey Council; Harrow Council; Havering Council; Highlands Council; Hillingdon Council; Hounslow Council; Hull Council; Islington Council; Kensington & Chelsea Council; Kingston Council; Lambeth Council; Lancaster Council; Leeds Council; Leicester Council; Lewisham Council; Lincoln Council; Lisburn Council; Liverpool Council; Llanelli Council; Manchester Council; Merthyr Tydfil Council; Merton Council; Middlesbrough Council; Milton Keynes Council; Newcastle Council; Newham Council; Newport Council; Newry Council; North Lanarkshire Council; Norwich Council; Nottingham Council; Oxford Council; Perth & Kinross Council; Peterborough Council; Plymouth Council; Portsmouth Council; Preston Council; Redbridge Council; Renfrewshire Council; Rhondda Cynon Taf Council; Richmond Council; Salford Council; Sheffield Council; South Lanarkshire Council; Southampton Council; Southend-on-Sea Council; Southwark Council; St. Albans Council; St. Asaph Council; St. Davids Council; Stirling Council; Stoke Council; Sunderland Council; Sutton Council; Swansea Council; Swindon Council; Tower Hamlets Council; Wakefield Council; Waltham Forest Council; Wandsworth Council; Warrington Council; West Lothian Council; Westminster Council; Winchester Council; Wolverhampton Council; Worcester Council; Wrexham Council; York Council

**From** Gerald Mclaverty

**Cc Bcc**

**Subject** Homelessness

Dear Council,

Please answer the following questions:
(I am a homeless person without any money)

Where can I go for something to eat or drink?
Where can I find shelter when it is raining or snowing?
Where can I go to a toilet during the day?
Where can I go to a toilet during the night?
Where can I get a bath or shower?
Where can I get clothes, footwear and a blanket?
Where can I wash my clothes?
Where can I sleep during the night that is safe?
Where can I go to use a computer?
Where can I go to use a telephone?
Where can I go to see a doctor?
Where can I go to see a dentist?
Where can I access facilities for my pet dog (food, bags for waste, vetcare)?

Thank you very much.

Gerald Mclaverty

**Send**

# /* UK COUNCILS */

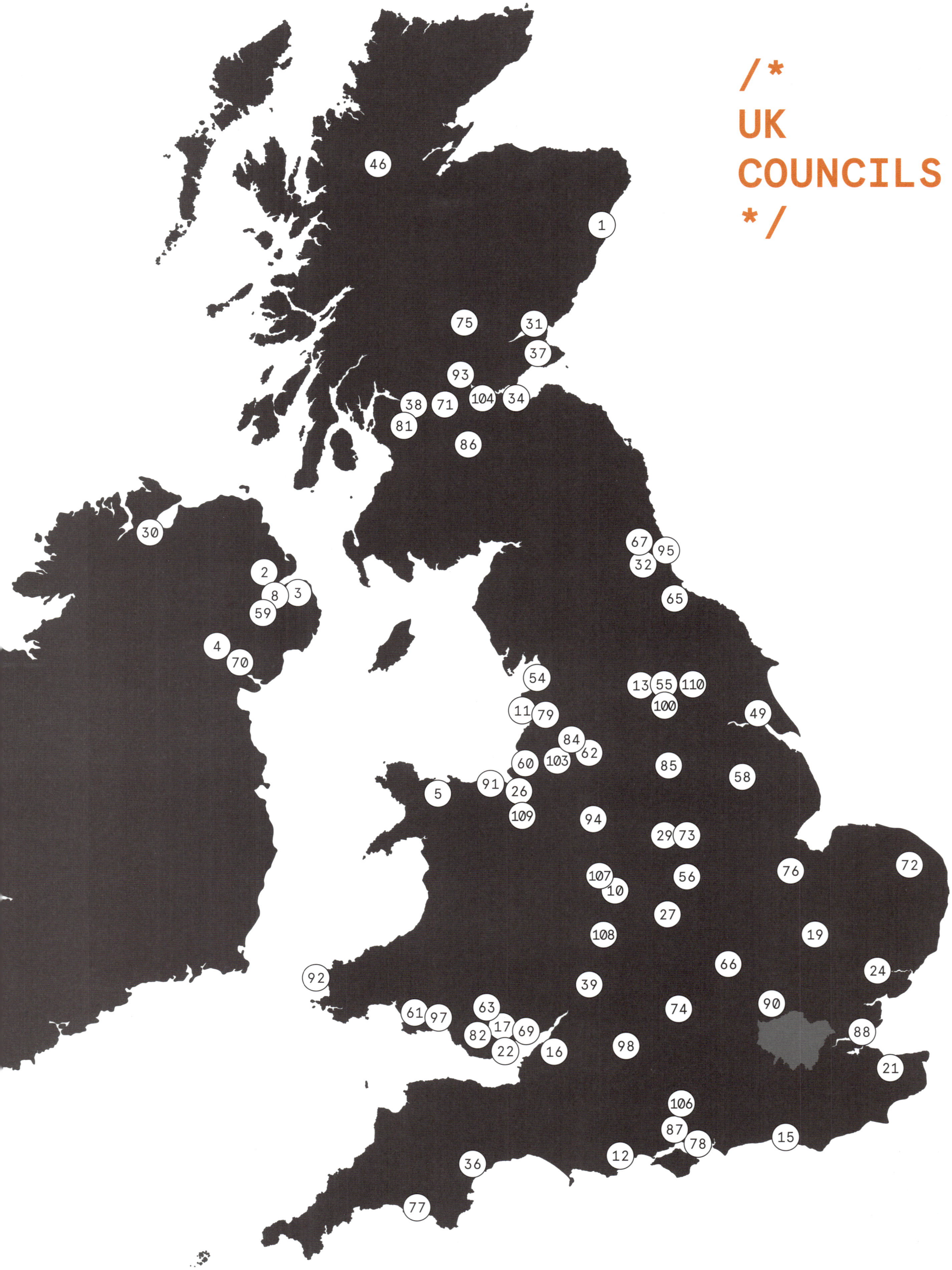
46
1
75
31
37
93
38
71
104
34
81
86
30
67
95
32
2
8
3
59
65
4
70
54
13
55
110
100
11
79
49
84
62
60
103
85
58
5
91
26
109
94
29
73
76
72
107
10
56
27
108
19
66
24
92
39
63
61
97
90
74
17
69
82
88
22
16
98
21
106
87
78
15
12
36
77

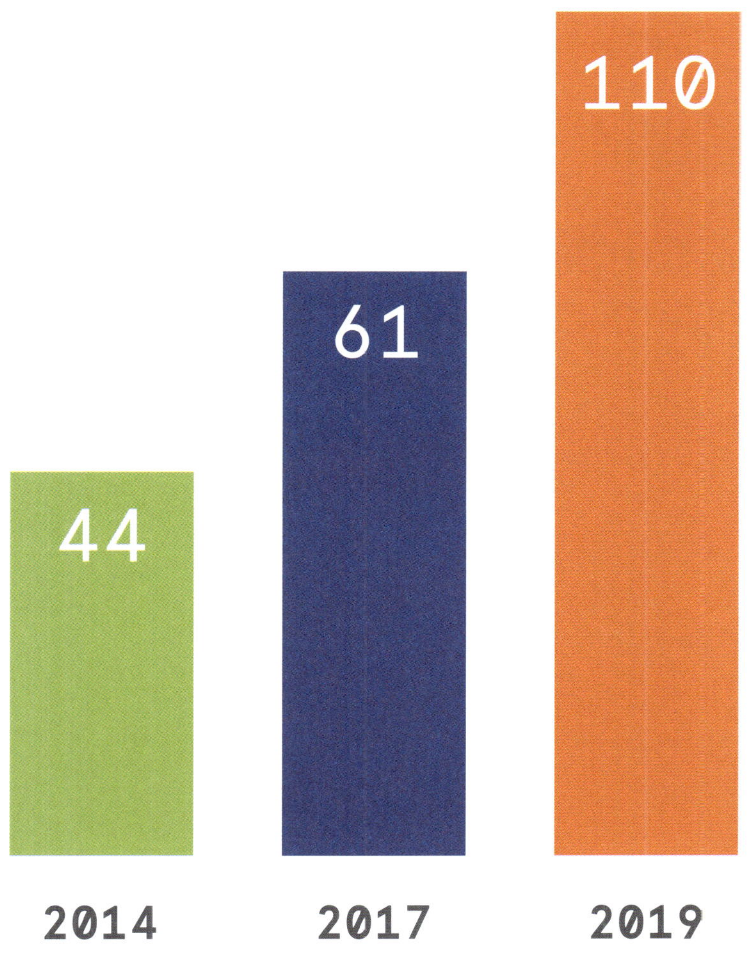


/*
EMAILS
SENT
*/

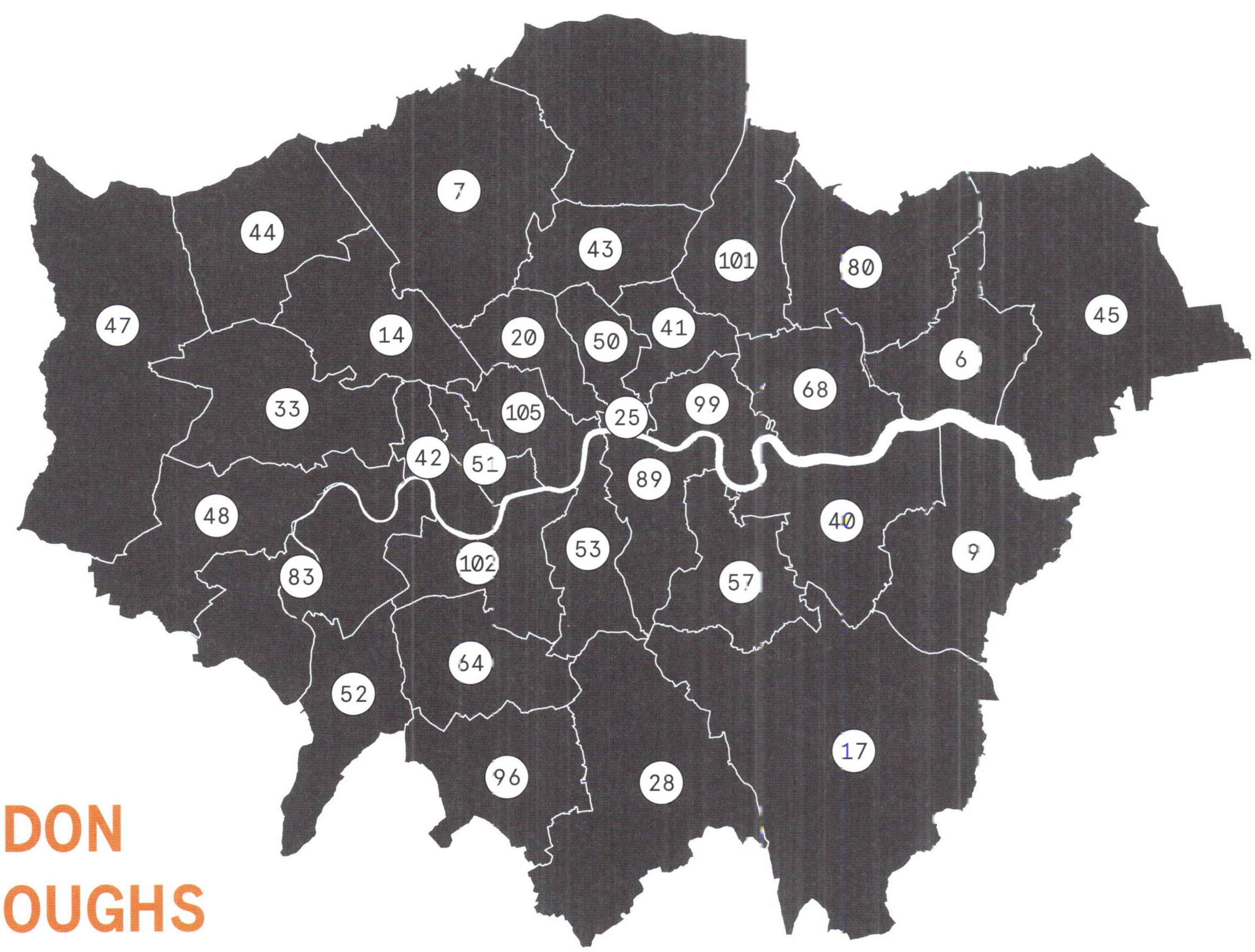


/*
LONDON
BOROUGHS
*/

# 2019

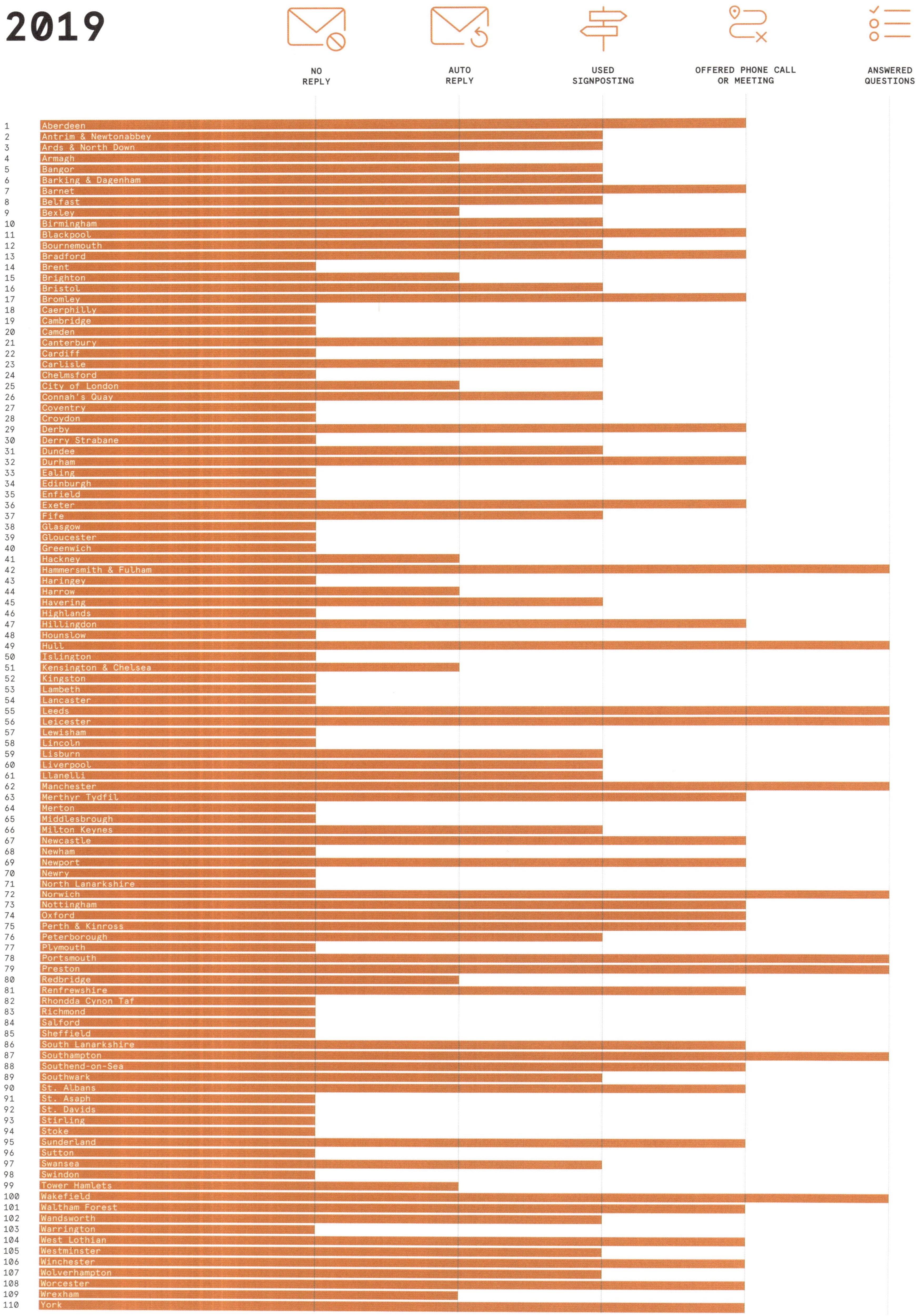
NO REPLY
AUTO REPLY
USED SIGNPOSTING
OFFERED PHONE CALL OR MEETING
ANSWERED QUESTIONS
1 Aberdeen
2 Antrim & Newtonabbey
3 Ards & North Down
4 Armagh
5 Bangor
6 Barking & Dagenham
7 Barnet
8 Belfast
9 Bexley
10 Birmingham
11 Blackpool
12 Bournemouth
13 Bradford
14 Brent
15 Brighton
16 Bristol
17 Bromley
18 Caerphilly
19 Cambridge
20 Camden
21 Canterbury
22 Cardiff
23 Carlisle
24 Chelmsford
25 City of London
26 Connah's Quay
27 Coventry
28 Croydon
29 Derby
30 Derry Strabane
31 Dundee
32 Durham
33 Ealing
34 Edinburgh
35 Enfield
36 Exeter
37 Fife
38 Glasgow
39 Gloucester
40 Greenwich
41 Hackney
42 Hammersmith & Fulham
43 Haringey
44 Harrow
45 Havering
46 Highlands
47 Hillingdon
48 Hounslow
49 Hull
50 Islington
51 Kensington & Chelsea
52 Kingston
53 Lambeth
54 Lancaster
55 Leeds
56 Leicester
57 Lewisham
58 Lincoln
59 Lisburn
60 Liverpool
61 Llanelli
62 Manchester
63 Merthyr Tydfil
64 Merton
65 Middlesbrough
66 Milton Keynes
67 Newcastle
68 Newham
69 Newport
70 Newry
71 North Lanarkshire
72 Norwich
73 Nottingham
74 Oxford
75 Perth & Kinross
76 Peterborough
77 Plymouth
78 Portsmouth
79 Preston
80 Redbridge
81 Renfrewshire
82 Rhondda Cynon Taf
83 Richmond
84 Salford
85 Sheffield
86 South Lanarkshire
87 Southampton
88 Southend-on-Sea
89 Southwark
90 St. Albans
91 St. Asaph
92 St. Davids
93 Stirling
94 Stoke
95 Sunderland
96 Sutton
97 Swansea
98 Swindon
99 Tower Hamlets
100 Wakefield
101 Waltham Forest
102 Wandsworth
103 Warrington
104 West Lothian
105 Westminster
106 Winchester
107 Wolverhampton
108 Worcester
109 Wrexham
110 York

# 2017

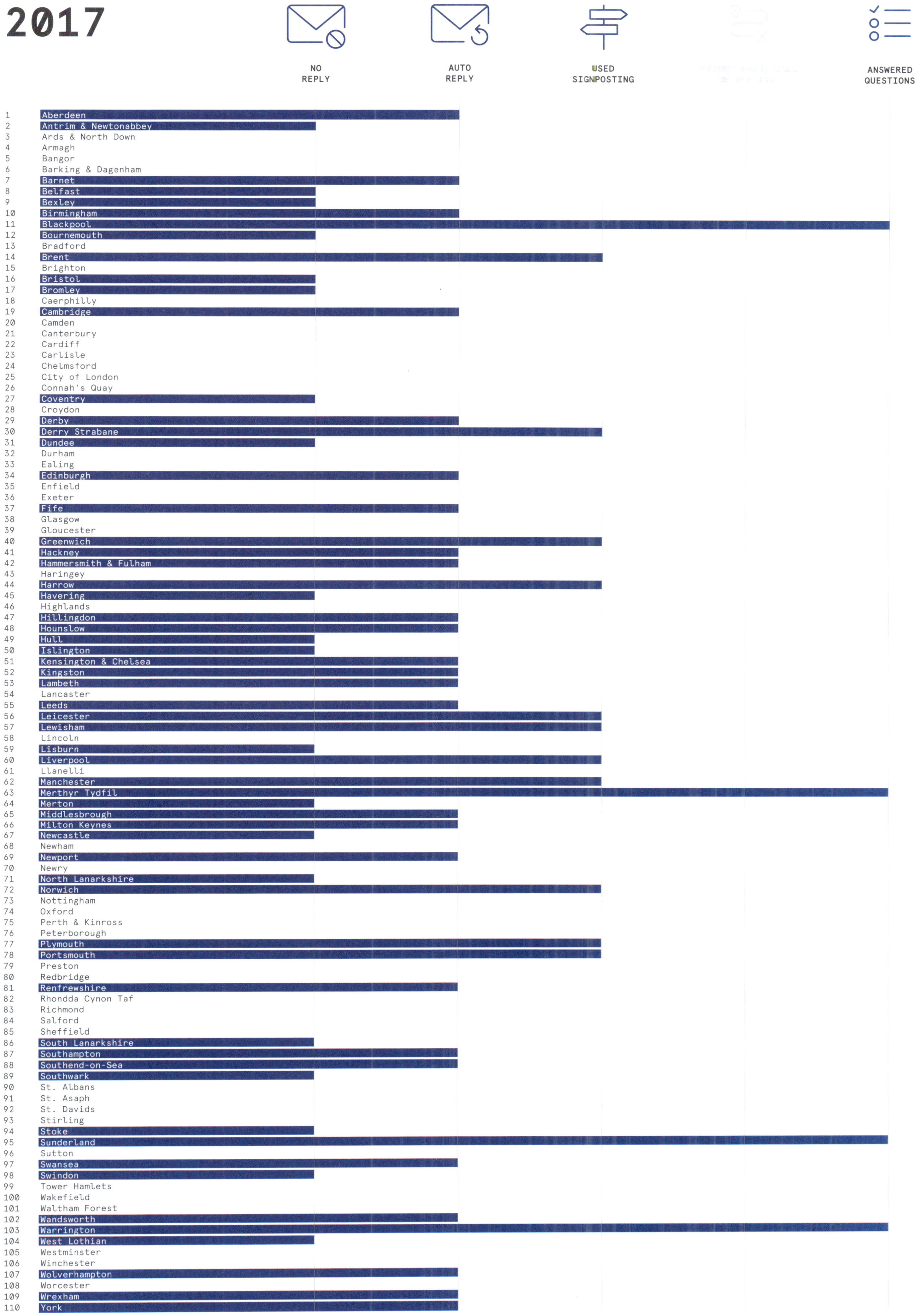
NO REPLY
AUTO REPLY
USED SIGNPOSTING
ANSWERED QUESTIONS
1 Aberdeen
2 Antrim & Newtonabbey
3 Ards & North Down
4 Armagh
5 Bangor
6 Barking & Dagenham
7 Barnet
8 Belfast
9 Bexley
10 Birmingham
11 Blackpool
12 Bournemouth
13 Bradford
14 Brent
15 Brighton
16 Bristol
17 Bromley
18 Caerphilly
19 Cambridge
20 Camden
21 Canterbury
22 Cardiff
23 Carlisle
24 Chelmsford
25 City of London
26 Connah's Quay
27 Coventry
28 Croydon
29 Derby
30 Derry Strabane
31 Dundee
32 Durham
33 Ealing
34 Edinburgh
35 Enfield
36 Exeter
37 Fife
38 Glasgow
39 Gloucester
40 Greenwich
41 Hackney
42 Hammersmith & Fulham
43 Haringey
44 Harrow
45 Havering
46 Highlands
47 Hillingdon
48 Hounslow
49 Hull
50 Islington
51 Kensington & Chelsea
52 Kingston
53 Lambeth
54 Lancaster
55 Leeds
56 Leicester
57 Lewisham
58 Lincoln
59 Lisburn
60 Liverpool
61 Llanelli
62 Manchester
63 Merthyr Tydfil
64 Merton
65 Middlesbrough
66 Milton Keynes
67 Newcastle
68 Newham
69 Newport
70 Newry
71 North Lanarkshire
72 Norwich
73 Nottingham
74 Oxford
75 Perth & Kinross
76 Peterborough
77 Plymouth
78 Portsmouth
79 Preston
80 Redbridge
81 Renfrewshire
82 Rhondda Cynon Taf
83 Richmond
84 Salford
85 Sheffield
86 South Lanarkshire
87 Southampton
88 Southend-on-Sea
89 Southwark
90 St. Albans
91 St. Asaph
92 St. Davids
93 Stirling
94 Stoke
95 Sunderland
96 Sutton
97 Swansea
98 Swindon
99 Tower Hamlets
100 Wakefield
101 Waltham Forest
102 Wandsworth
103 Warrington
104 West Lothian
105 Westminster
106 Winchester
107 Wolverhampton
108 Worcester
109 Wrexham
110 York

# 2014

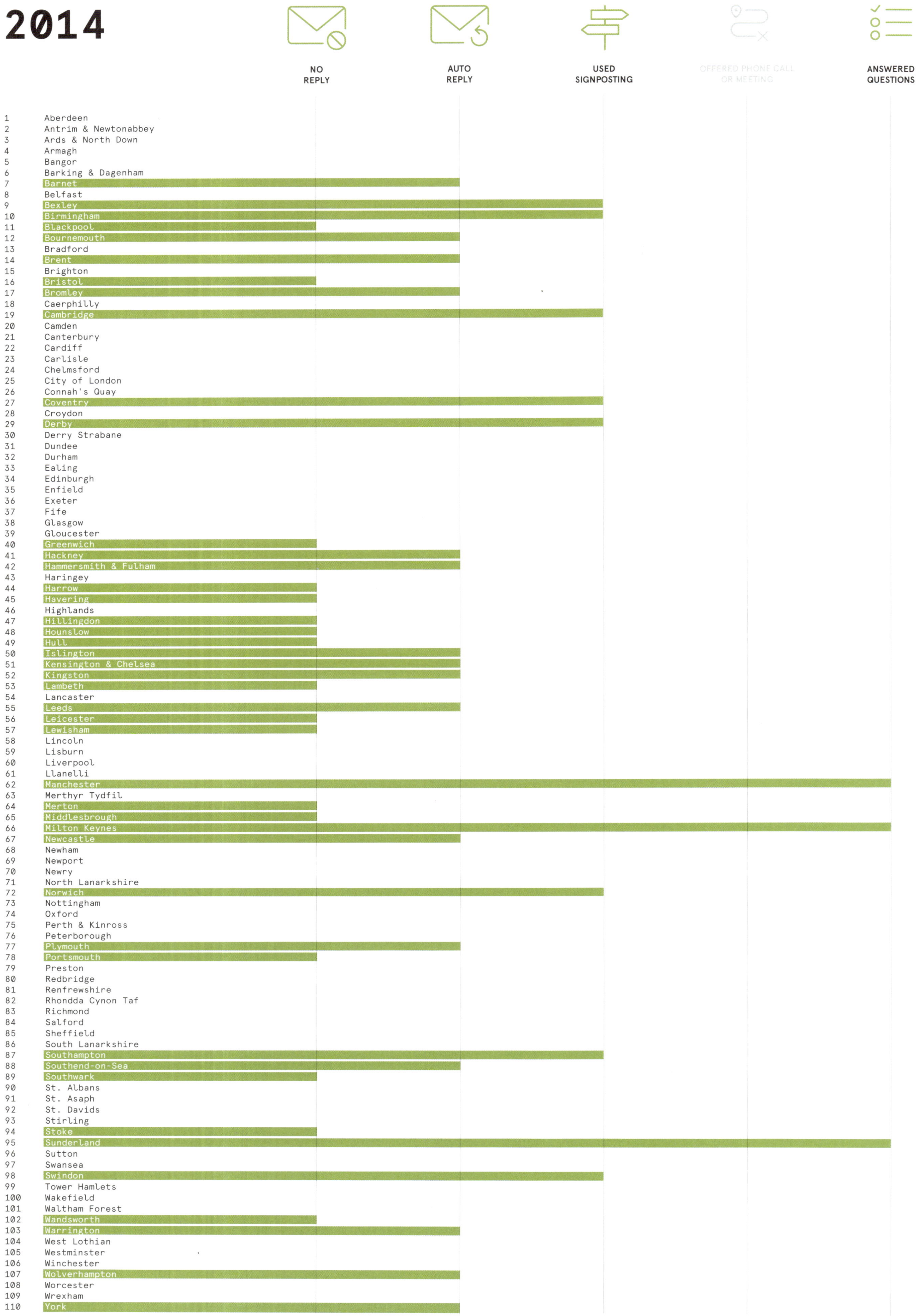
NO REPLY
AUTO REPLY
USED SIGNPOSTING
OFFERED PHONE CALL OR MEETING
ANSWERED QUESTIONS
1 Aberdeen
2 Antrim & Newtonabbey
3 Ards & North Down
4 Armagh
5 Bangor
6 Barking & Dagenham
7 Barnet
8 Belfast
9 Bexley
10 Birmingham
11 Blackpool
12 Bournemouth
13 Bradford
14 Brent
15 Brighton
16 Bristol
17 Bromley
18 Caerphilly
19 Cambridge
20 Camden
21 Canterbury
22 Cardiff
23 Carlisle
24 Chelmsford
25 City of London
26 Connah's Quay
27 Coventry
28 Croydon
29 Derby
30 Derry Strabane
31 Dundee
32 Durham
33 Ealing
34 Edinburgh
35 Enfield
36 Exeter
37 Fife
38 Glasgow
39 Gloucester
40 Greenwich
41 Hackney
42 Hammersmith & Fulham
43 Haringey
44 Harrow
45 Havering
46 Highlands
47 Hillingdon
48 Hounslow
49 Hull
50 Islington
51 Kensington & Chelsea
52 Kingston
53 Lambeth
54 Lancaster
55 Leeds
56 Leicester
57 Lewisham
58 Lincoln
59 Lisburn
60 Liverpool
61 Llanelli
62 Manchester
63 Merthyr Tydfil
64 Merton
65 Middlesbrough
66 Milton Keynes
67 Newcastle
68 Newham
69 Newport
70 Newry
71 North Lanarkshire
72 Norwich
73 Nottingham
74 Oxford
75 Perth & Kinross
76 Peterborough
77 Plymouth
78 Portsmouth
79 Preston
80 Redbridge
81 Renfrewshire
82 Rhondda Cynon Taf
83 Richmond
84 Salford
85 Sheffield
86 South Lanarkshire
87 Southampton
88 Southend-on-Sea
89 Southwark
90 St. Albans
91 St. Asaph
92 St. Davids
93 Stirling
94 Stoke
95 Sunderland
96 Sutton
97 Swansea
98 Swindon
99 Tower Hamlets
100 Wakefield
101 Waltham Forest
102 Wandsworth
103 Warrington
104 West Lothian
105 Westminster
106 Winchester
107 Wolverhampton
108 Worcester
109 Wrexham
110 York

/*
# NO REPLY
*/

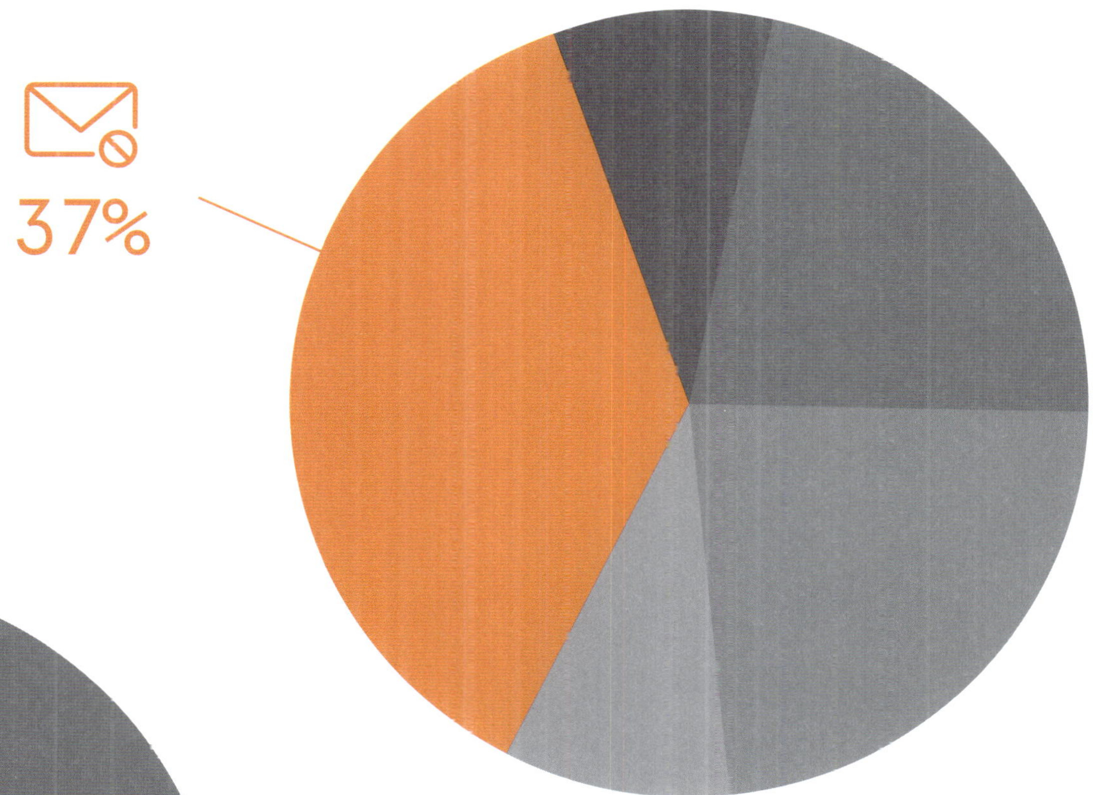


2019

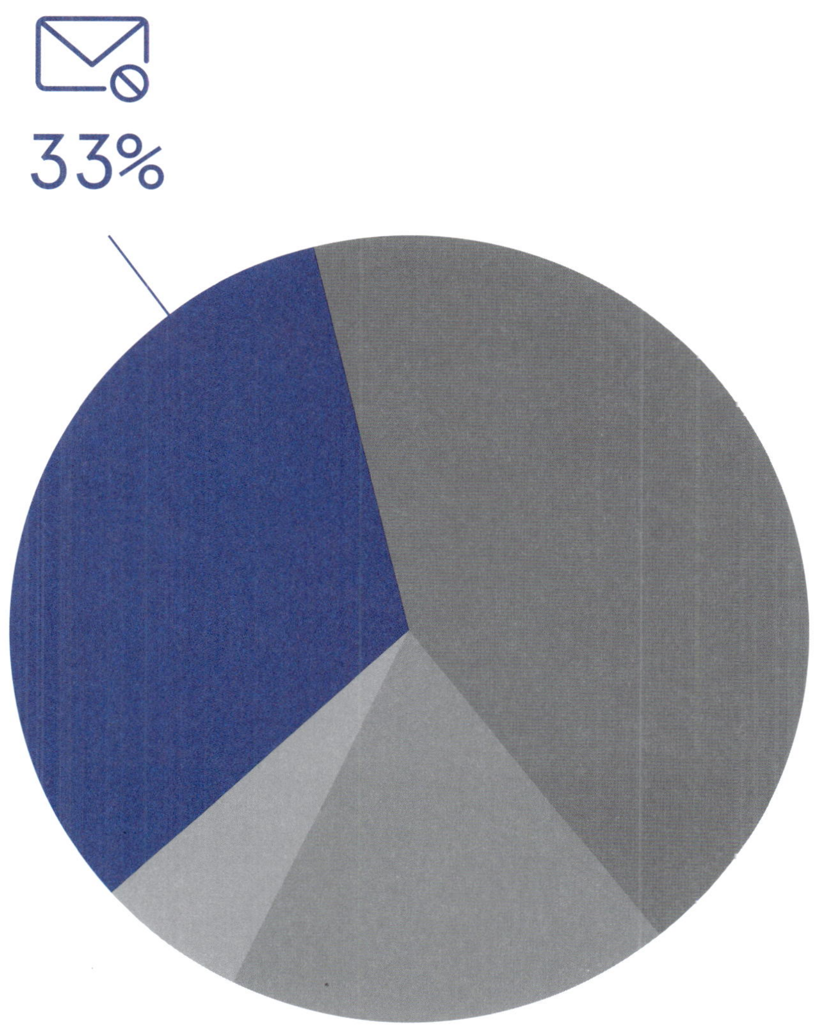


2017

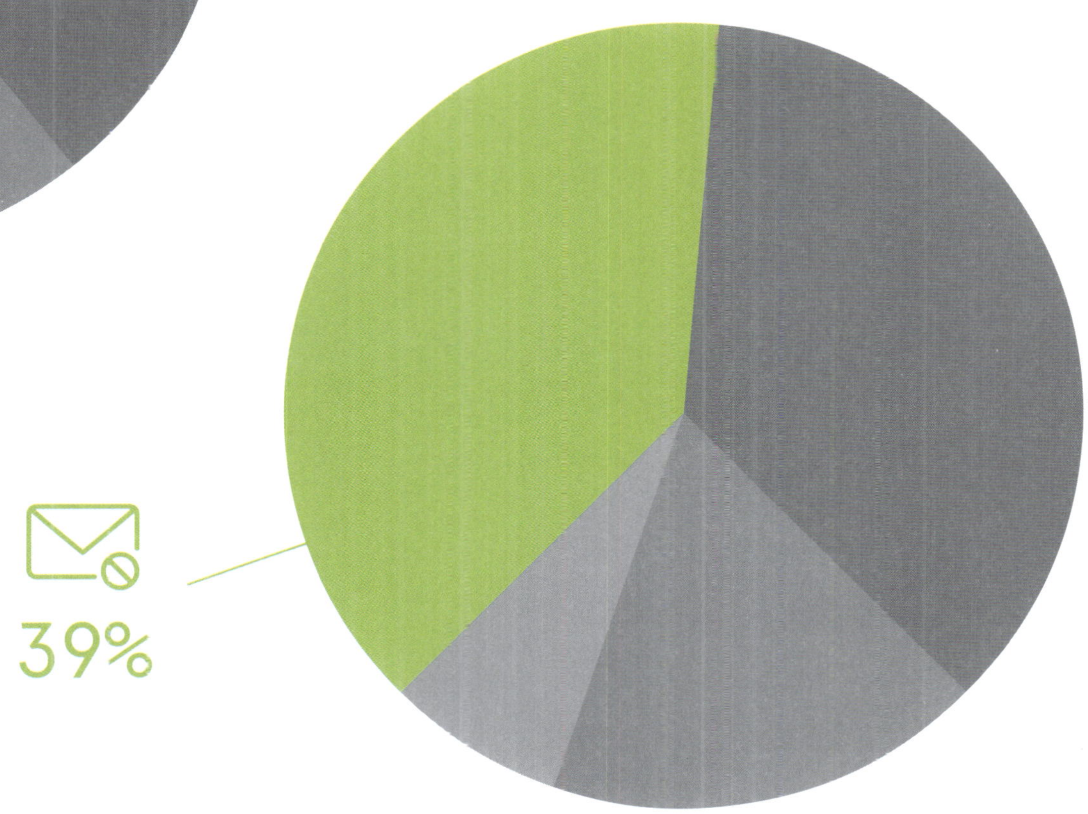


2014

/*
# AUTO REPLY
*/

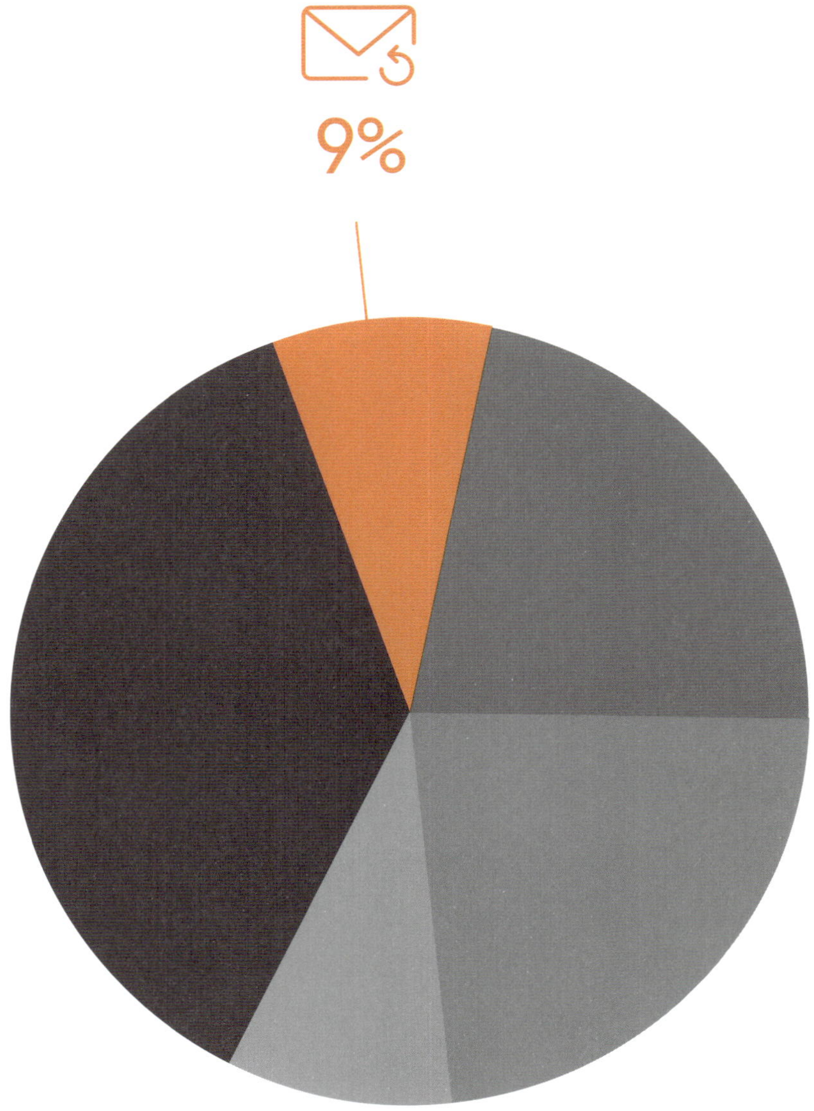


2019

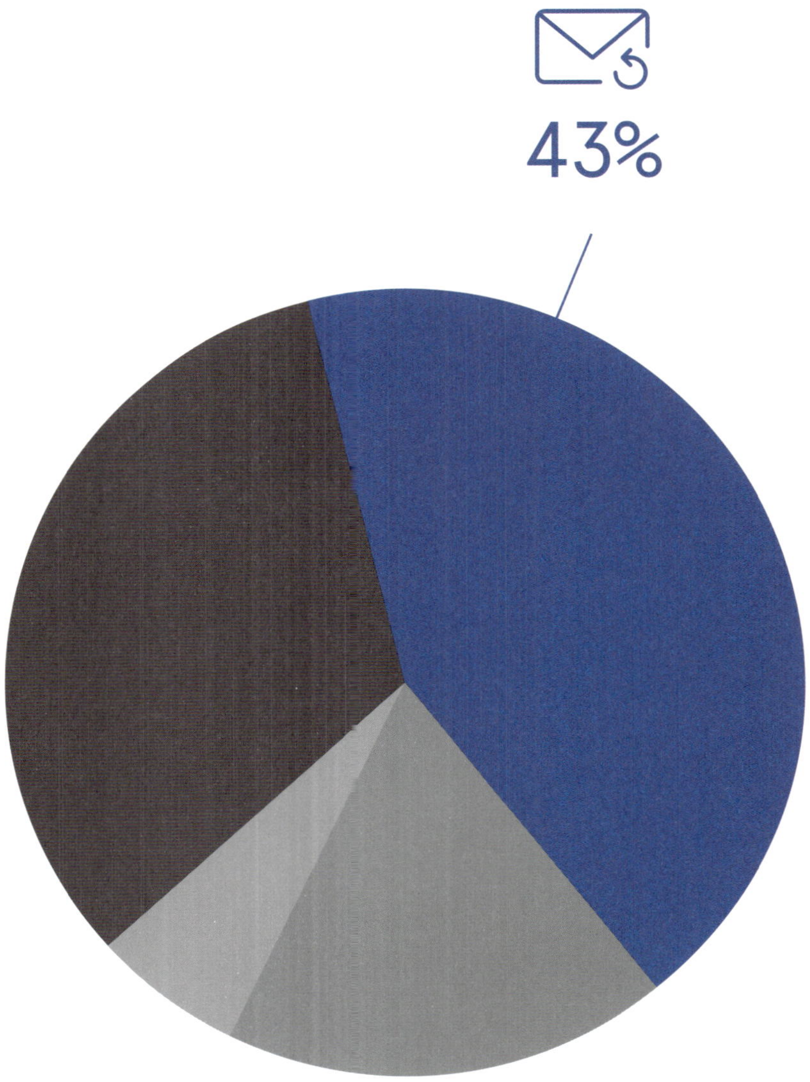


2017

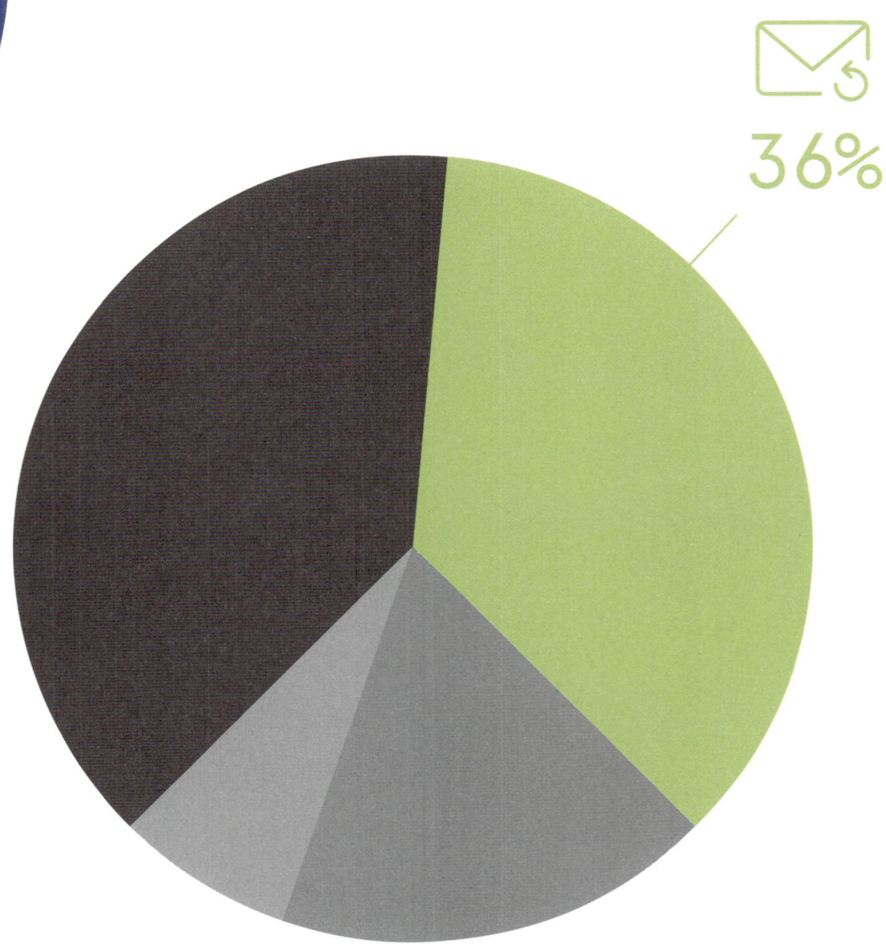


2014

## /* NO REPLY */

**In 2019, 41 councils did not reply:**

Brent, Caerphilly, Cambridge, Camden, Cardiff, Chelmsford, Coventry, Croydon, Derry and Strabane, Ealing, Edinburgh, Enfield, Glasgow, Gloucester, Greenwich, Haringey, Highland, Hounslow, Islington, Kingston, Lambeth, Lancaster, Lewisham, Lincoln, Merton, Middlesbrough, Newham, Newry, North Lanarkshire, Plymouth, Rhondda Cynon Taf, Richmond upon Thames, Salford, Sheffield, St Asaph, St Davids, Stirling, Stoke-on-Trent, Sutton, Swindon, Warrington

## /* AUTO REPLY */

**In 2019, 35 councils replied with an automated email:**

Ards and North Down, Armagh City, Barking and Dagenham, Barnet, Bexley, Birmingham, Brighton and Hove, Bromley, Carlisle, Swansea, Canterbury, City of London, Derby, Durham, Exeter, Fife, Hackney, Hammersmith and Fulham, Harrow, Kensington and Chelsea, Leeds, Leicester, Lisburn and Castlereagh, Liverpool, Manchester, Milton Keynes, Perth and Kinross, Redbridge, Southampton, Tower Hamlets, West Lothian, Wolverhampton, Worcester, Wrexham, York

## /* USED SIGNPOSTING */

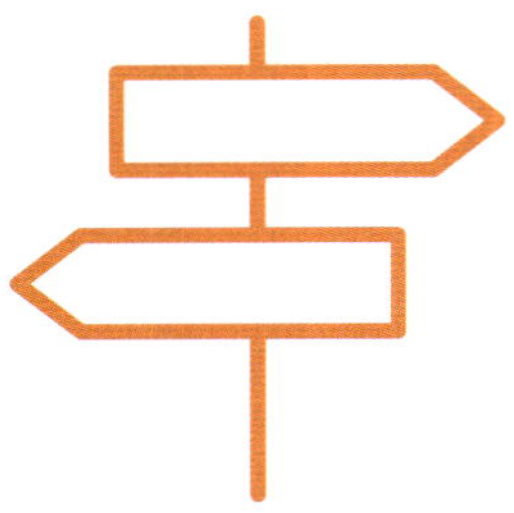

**In 2019, 30 councils signposted to websites about housing or homelessness:**

Antrim and Newtownabbey, Ards & North Down, Bangor, Barking and Dagenham, Belfast, Birmingham, Bournemouth, Bristol, Canterbury, Carlisle, Connah's Quay, Dundee, Fife, Havering, Hull, Leeds, Leicester, Lisburn, Liverpool, Llanelli, Manchester, Milton Keynes, Peterborough, Preston, Southampton, Southwark, Swansea, Wandsworth, Westminster, Wolverhampton

## /* RESPONSE TIMES */

**In 2019, 24 councils replied with an automated email that promised a follow up within a certain timeframe.**

| | |
|---|---|
| **24 hrs** | Brighton, Manchester, West Lothian |
| **2 days** | Durham, Kensington and Chelsea, Liverpool, Perth, Southampton |
| **3 days** | Carlisle |
| **5 days** | Barnet, Bromley, Derby, Fife, Harrow, Leeds, Wrexham |
| **10 days** | Birmingham, Swansea, City of London, Hackney, Redbridge, Tower Hamlets, York |
| **14 days** | Canterbury |

**Only 15 councils honoured their response time pledge.**

/*

# USED SIGNPOSTING

*/

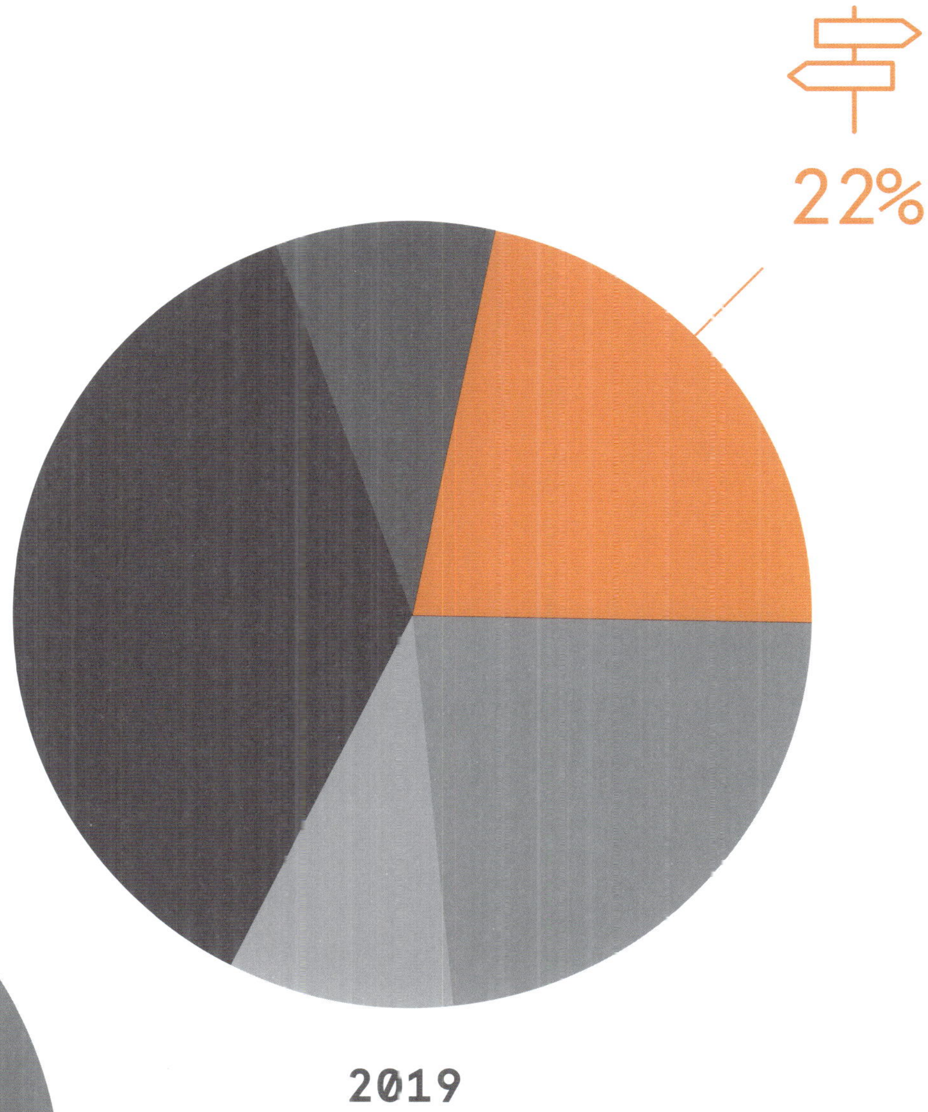


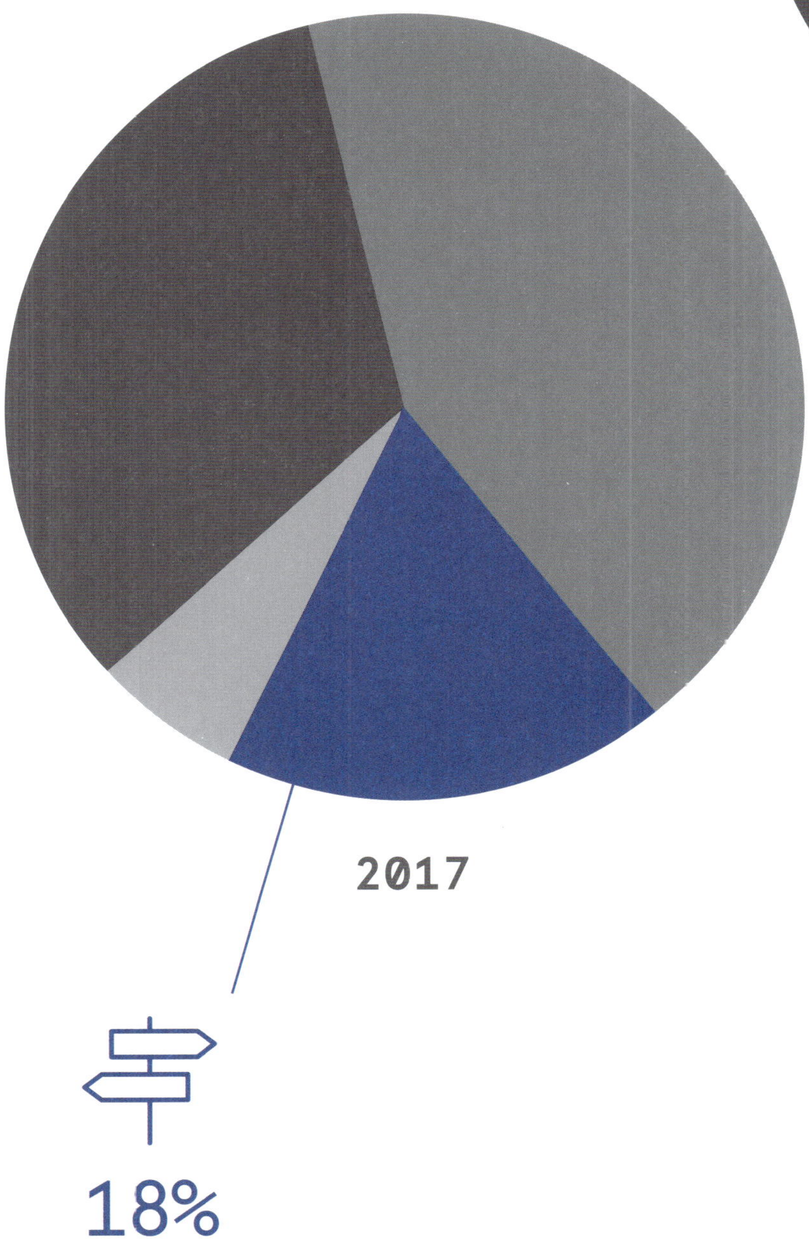


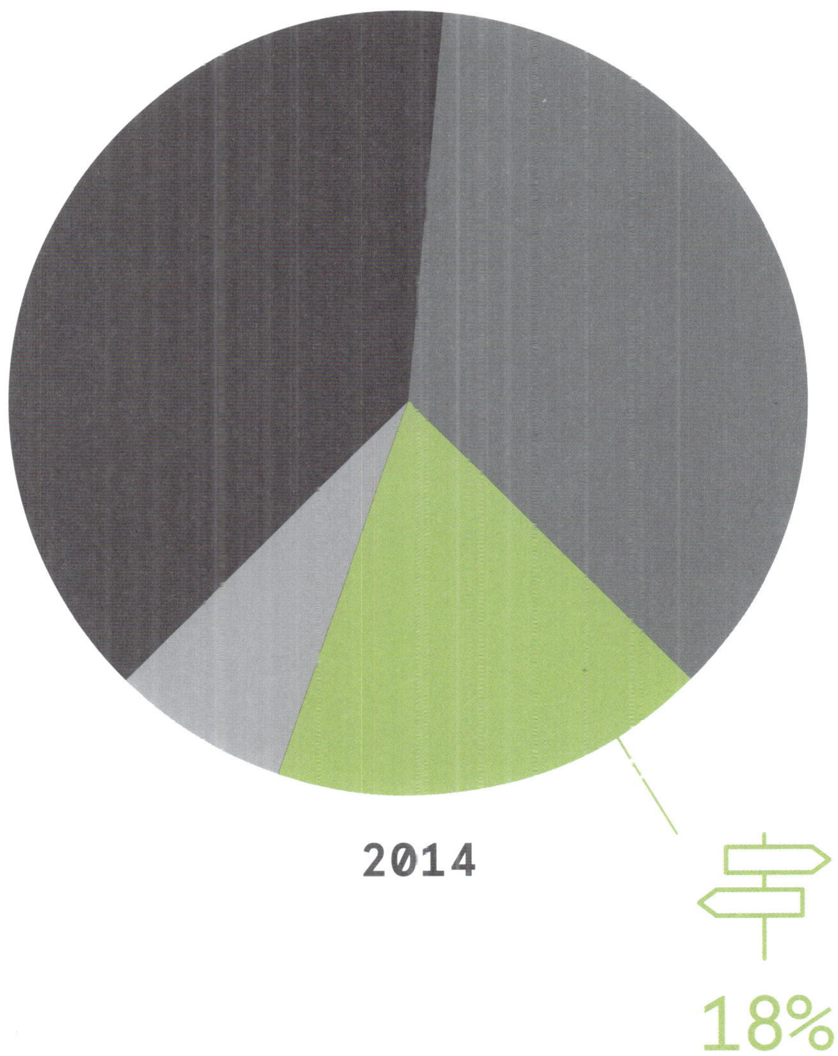

/*
# ANSWERED QUESTIONS
*/

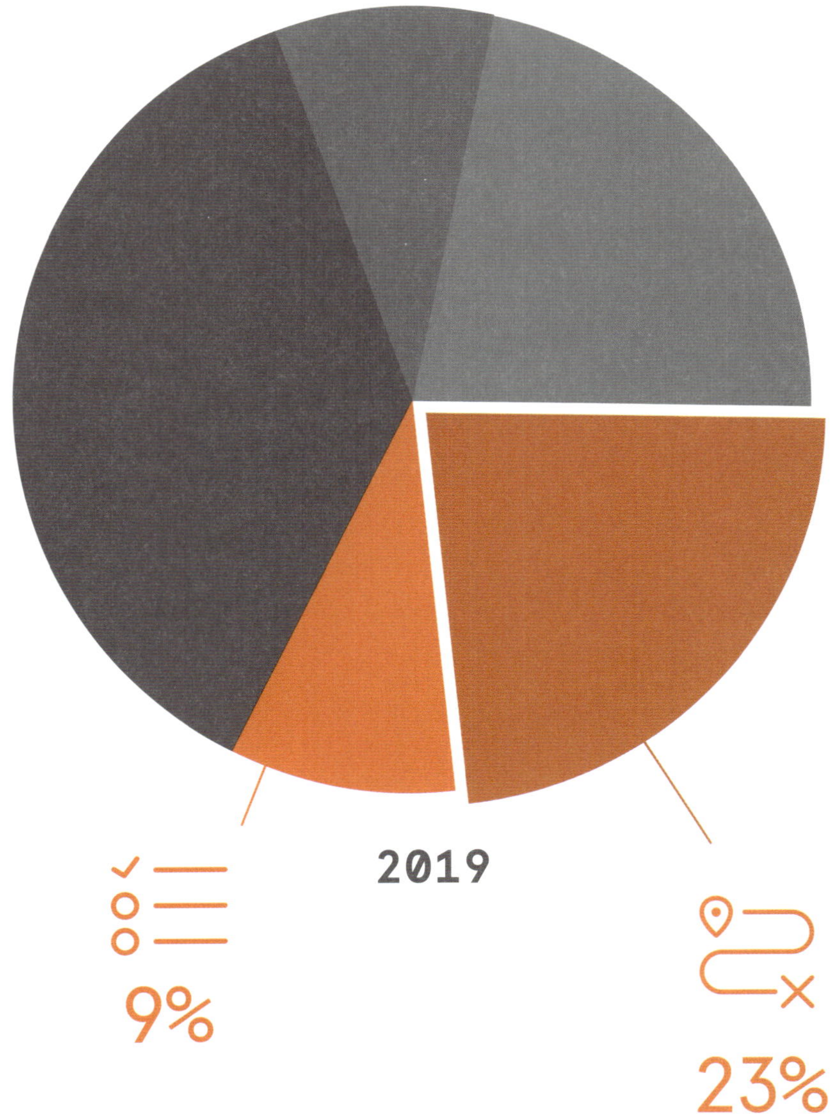


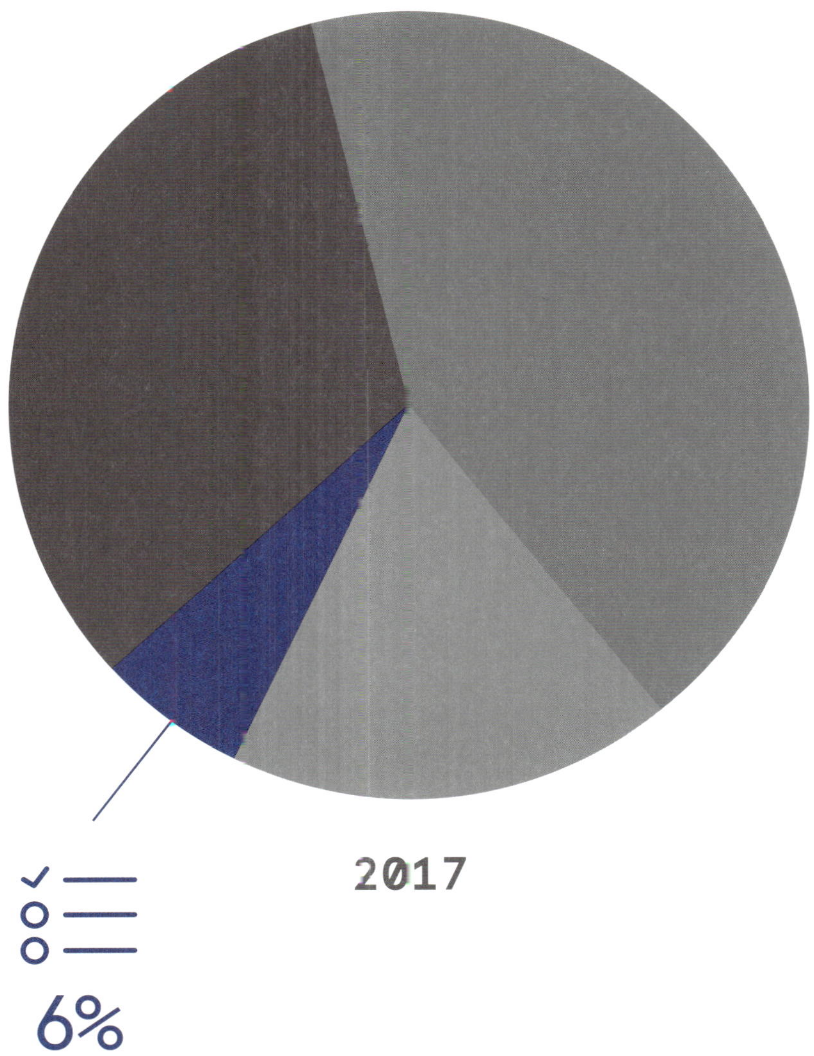


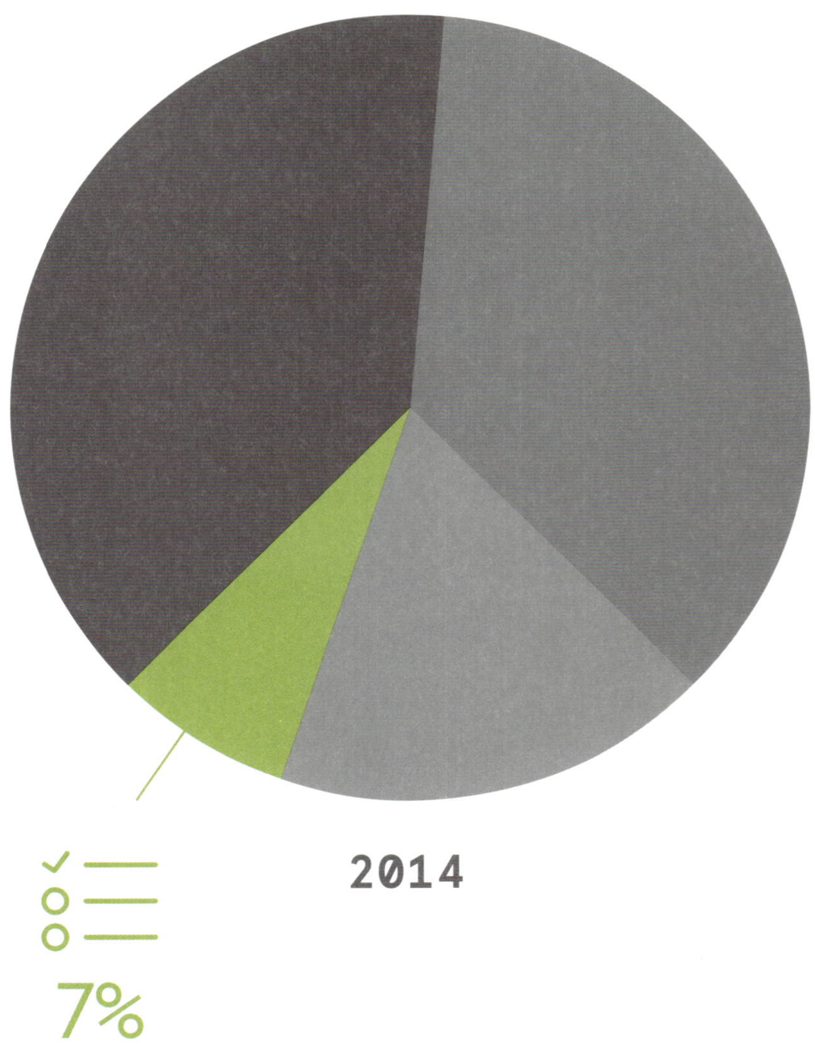

# /* ROLES, TEAMS & DEPARTMENTS */

**The enquiry was sent to homelessness and housing support listed on council websites, responses came back from the following:**

Administrative Assistant, Administrative Team, Applications Officer, Area Housing Manager, Assistant Homelessness Services Manager, Business Support Officer, Customer Service Advisor, Customer Services, Customer Services Team, Duty Officer, Gateway Customer Service Officer, General Enquiries Helpdesk, Graduate Trainee, Housing Advice Department, Home and Money Department, Homeless Outreach & Support Worker, Homeless Prevention, Homelessness Prevention Assistant, Homelessness Prevention Officer, Housing Advice, Housing Advice Assistant, Housing Advice Line, Housing Advice Officer, Housing Advice Service, Housing Advisor, Housing Aid, Housing Assessment and Advice Officer, Housing Assistant, Housing Caseworker, Housing Department, Housing Needs Gateway Officer, Housing Needs Officer, Housing Operations, Housing Options, Housing Options Assistant, Housing Options Duty, Housing Options Officer, Housing Options Officer, Homeless Team, Housing Options Team, Housing Options Worker, Housing Solution Service, Housing Solutions, Housing Team, Officer Manager, Official, P3 Outreach, Rough Sleeper Administrative Assistant, Rough Sleeper Outreach Team, Rough Sleepers, Senior Customer Services Officer, Specialist Caseworker, Street Homeless Support Worker, Street Homeless Support Worker, Housing Solutions Team, Team Manager, Housing Options Service, Town Clerk

# /* EXCERPTS FROM RESPONSES */

Homelessness Autoresponder
- please do not reply.

We will normally respond to requests for advice and information within 2 working days.

You may find the information you are looking for at our website

Best Regards,

Dear Housing customer,

Thank you for contacting the Housing Options Team, your enquiry will be looked at within the next 24 hours and we will get back to you within 10 working days at the latest.

Regards

Housing Services

***
Please do not reply to this email address as this is an automated response
***

Thank you for your email referral for a household who is at risk of homelessness within 56 days.

We will make contact with the person(s) referred using the contact information you have supplied within 3 working days.

If the household has nowhere to sleep tonight, please advise them to come to the civic centre as a matter of urgency or contact us on [redacted] (during office hours).

Thank you for contacting [redacted] City Council Customer Services. You can visit www.[redacted].gov.uk for more information, including bin collections dates and reporting missed bins, as well as setting up your online Council Tax account.

In case of an emergency, please call [redacted].

Yours sincerely

Customer Service Team

Thank you for your email.

If you are a customer, we will aim to respond to your email within 2 working days.

Thank you for your email.

We are currently experiencing a high volume of emails and aim to reply to you within 48 hours.

Good Afternoon,

Do you have a contact number that I can ring you on to discuss your homeless issues and to see how [redacted] can assist you.

Your questions cannot be answered unless we are aware of the area you are at the moment.

Thanks

Housing Advice Line
Housing Solutions
Civic Centre

If you are homeless, I would advise that you come into [redacted] and see our Housing Options Team. They will look into your circumstances and give you your housing options once you have had an assessment.

Many thanks

Good Afternoon

With reference to your email detailed below, if you are homeless I would advise that you contact the Outreach Team on [redacted] as they will be able to help you.

Applications Officer
| Customer Services |
Business Improvements

I am sorry to read of your current housing situation. If [redacted] city council can be of assistance, you will need to complete a housing assessment form online at selfserve. [redacted].gov.uk or in person

Many Thanks
Housing Team

**************************
**************************
******************

[redacted] City Council
- delivering excellent services for [redacted]

**************************
**************************

All correspondence will be dealt with in date order however there will be a delay in responding. We ask that you do not email for further updates as to the progress of your enquiry as the team will contact you once they have completed your assessment. Your patience during this time would be appreciated.

---

We aim to contact your client within 2 working days. We may need to contact you if we need additional information.

Our duty service can be contacted on [redacted]. Please note that we are open 9am - 5pm Monday to Friday.

Regards

Housing and Homelessness Assessment Team

---

Thank you for your email which will be passed to the relevant officer for response. We respond to all correspondence within 10 working days but will reply to urgent enquiries as quickly as possible.

---

Dear Mr. Mclaverty

I am forwarding your enquiry on to [redacted] who is the Unitary Authority responsible.

Kind regards,

Office Manager

---

Hi there,

We are able to assist you. If you are under 25, our office is [redacted].
If you are over 25, it would be [redacted].

Our opening times are Monday to Thursday 8:45am to 4:45pm and on the Friday 8:45am to 3:55pm. A Housing Options interview will take about an hour. Please bring ID and proof of your income.

Kind regards,

Customer & Business Services

---

Dear Sir

Thank you for your email.

Your email does not contain enough information for us to register your request for assistance.

Please call us on [redacted] so we can capture more information and provide you with assistance.

Many thanks.

Can you advise if this is a freedom of information request? If so can you please look at our website for information how to request this.

Regards

---

Dear Mr McIlaverty,

Thank you for your correspondence.

To confirm I have passed your email onto the relevant department, who will deal with it in due course.

Kind regards,

Administrative Assistant: Performance and Audit

---

Hello,

If you are homeless in [redacted] and have a local connection to the city, then you can approach in person [redacted] City Council Housing Options Team.

Any further contact from you will require your date of birth, national insurance number and last fixed address or tenancy or care of postal address in order to give more specific responses and answers.

---

Hello

All I can suggest is that you contact Citizens Advice [redacted].

Regards

---

Prynhawn da/Good afternoon,

Thank you for your email.

You can declare yourself as a homeless person. Please go to the address below.

[redacted]

Opening hours:
Monday, Tuesday, Thursday and Friday 09:00-12:00 and 14:00-16:00
Cofion cynnes/Kind regards

---

Thank you for taking the time to contact [redacted] Borough Council.

Due to the current data protection legislation we unable to forward your query and details on to any external agencies unless you give written consent to do so. If you are having issues please do not hesitate to contact us to give this permission and we can forward your details on for you.

Kind Regards

Customer Services

Thank you for the submission.

What happens next?
Your form has been sent to the relevant department.
We will contact you if we need any more information.

This is a one-time email confirmation.

---

Hi,

Thanks for contacting us online. Your message has been received and if needed we will contact you back as soon as possible. You can always expect a reply within 14 working days, but in many cases it will be sooner than that.

---

Official

Please contact the [redacted] website for assistance as you state you are homeless and without money.

---

Thank you for your enquiry. This is an automatic confirmation that we have received your e-mail.

You will be receiving an email update on the progress of your enquiry within 5 working days.

---

Thank you for your email.

I have noted your comments and I would strongly advise you to contact the Home and Money Department

Kind Regards

---

Good day,

Sorry to hear about your current circumstance.

Are you sleeping rough?

If so, where are you currently sleeping where did you sleep last night.

Thank you

Kind Regards,
Gateway Customer Service Officer

---

Thanks for getting in touch

This is an automated response to let you know we received your message. We will contact you as soon as possible.

Thank you.

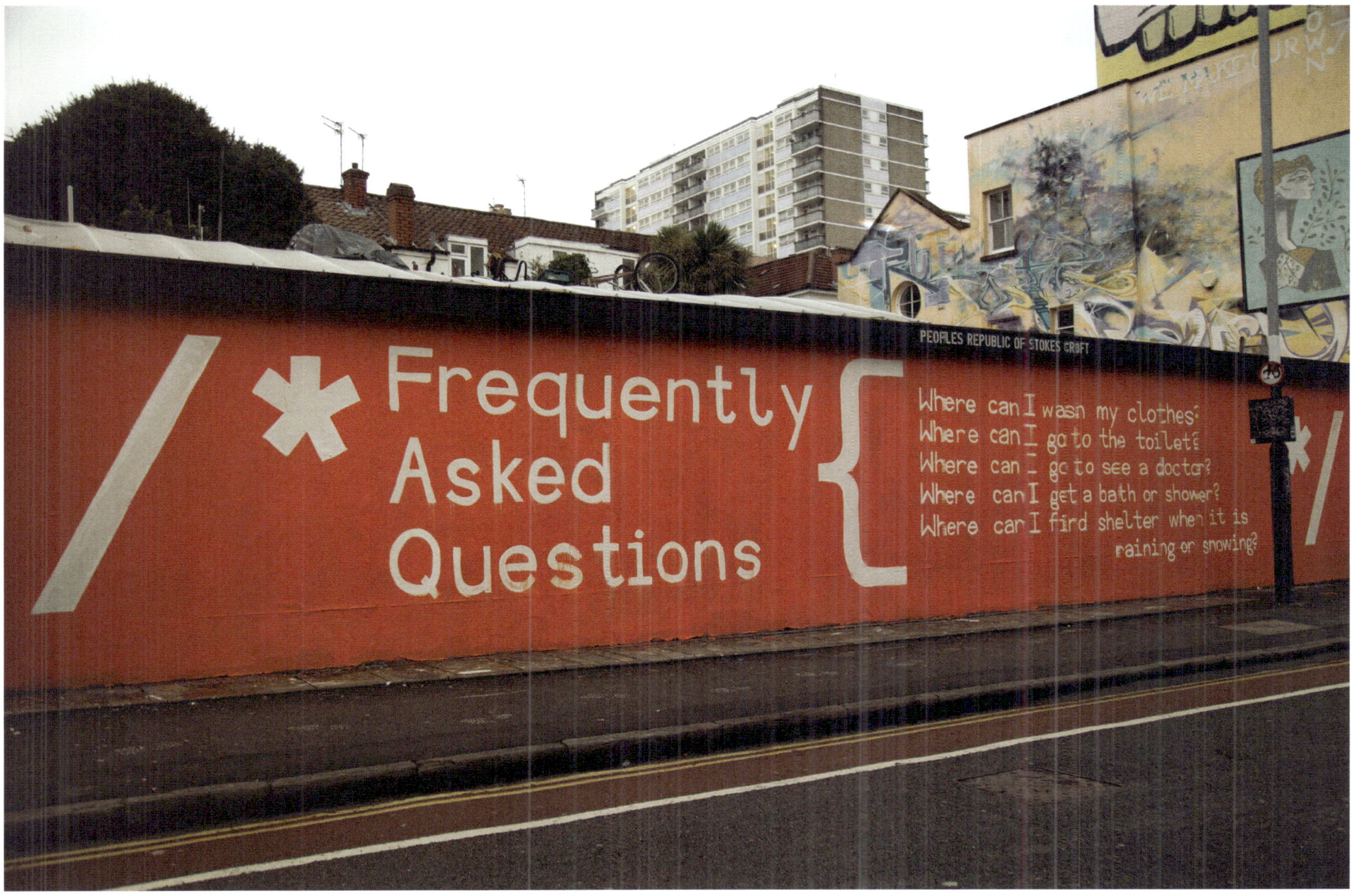


Frequently Asked Questions, People's Republic of Stokes Croft, Bristol,
27th November to 12th December 2019

# /* QUESTIONS ARE MORE IMPORTANT THAN EVER */

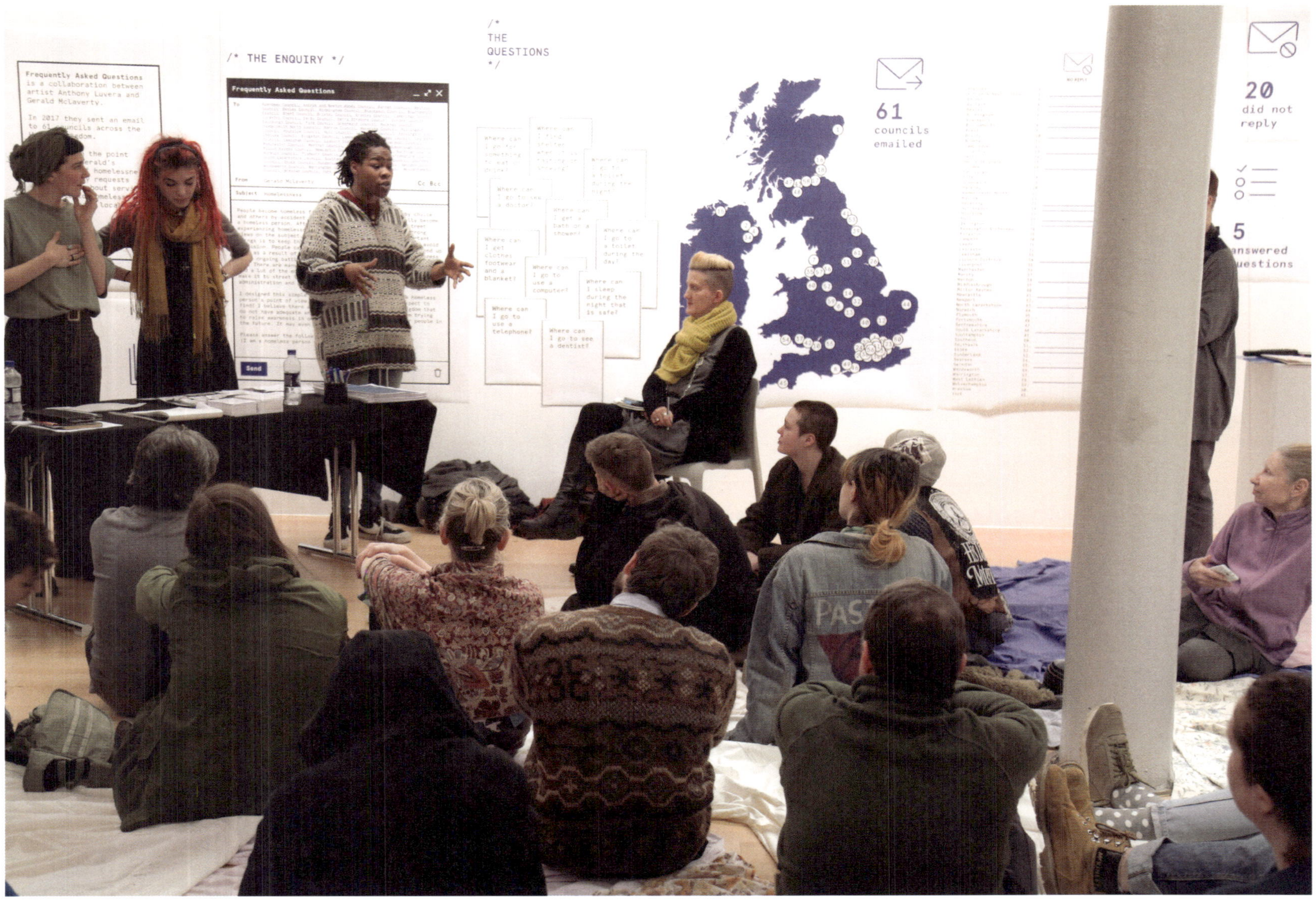


Workshop with Established Beyond, Frequently Asked Questions, State of the Nation with Museum of Homelessness, Tate Liverpool, 22nd to 28th January 2018

"The shock of understanding what the councils aren't doing to help, 92% of councils haven't even responded to questions about basic human needs… that we should all have the right to… profound, touching and upsetting."
- Visitor to Frequently Asked Questions at Tate Liverpool, 2018

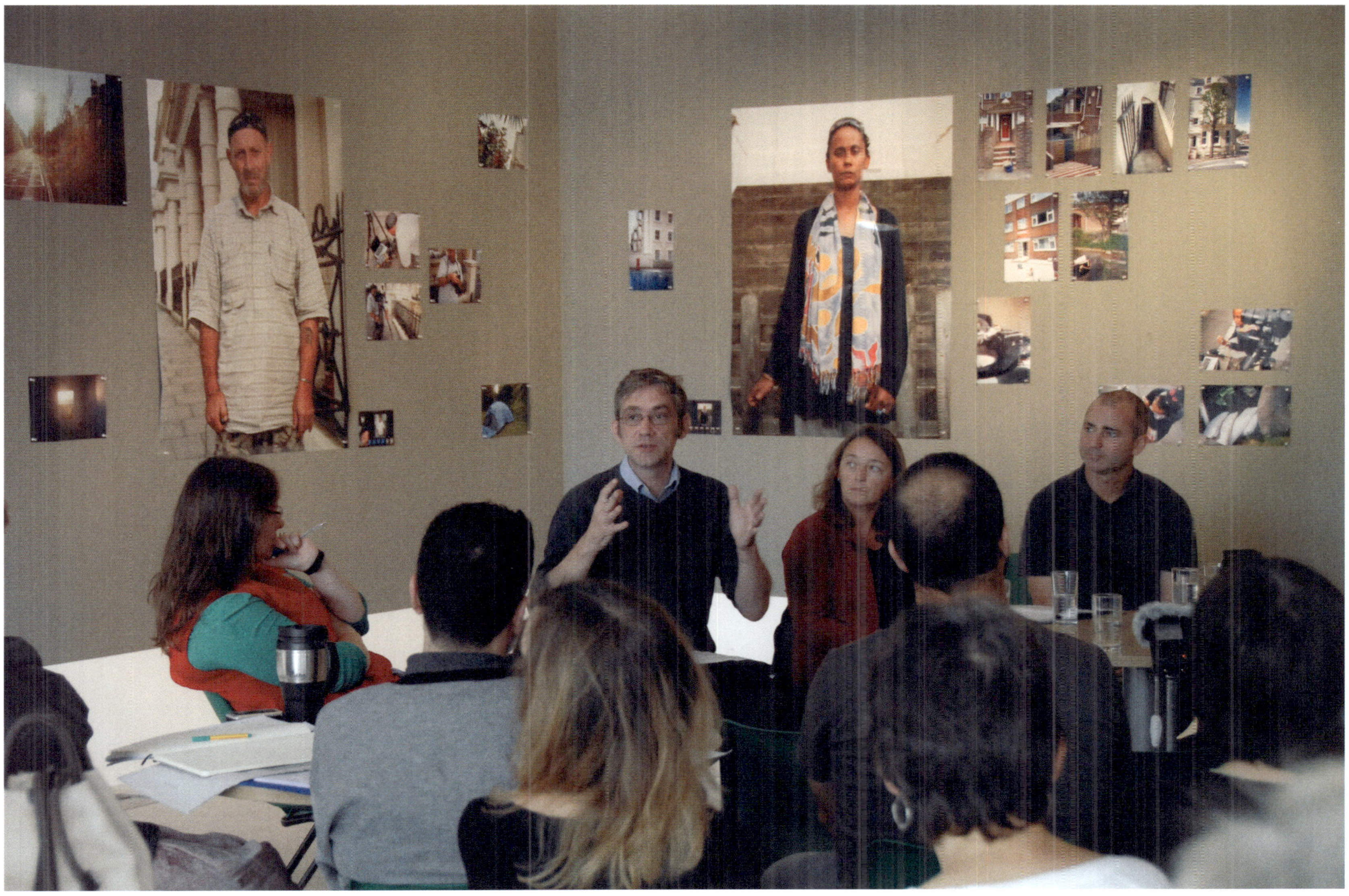

Panel discussion, Frequently Asked Questions, Assembly by Anthony Luvera, Brighton Photo Fringe, Phoenix Gallery, Brighton, 11th October 2014

If you emailed your local council asking questions related to your basic human rights, what would you expect in response? This provocation powerfully frames Frequently Asked Questions, a research-led artistic intervention created by Anthony Luvera and Gerald Mclaverty. The provocation puts you in the position of thinking through all the eventualities: If you were in crisis, what could you expect to encounter? A list of services swiftly emailed over or a link to a website? A personalised reply with a handy checklist that the council staff team has on standby for moments like these? Or perhaps to be connected with someone who can offer immediate help?

In fact, such obvious expectations barely correlate with reality. This offers us a first clue into how contacting local authorities with a set of basic questions about everyday survival can be such a potent piece of activism. It is at the heart of why Frequently Asked Questions works so well.

We remember meeting Anthony for the first time in 2016, when he showed us copies of the emails that were sent to councils in 2014. They went on forever, an endless set of auto-replies, referrals to departments with names like 'transformation services' and numerous cases where the council thought that the questions were a freedom of information request. It evidenced so strongly why there are so many people who have gone through homelessness who are deeply suspicious of the systems of care that are meant to support them. It made us immediately want to work with Anthony to stage the second instalment of the work as part of our yearlong State of the Nation season at Tate Liverpool in early 2018.

Frequently Asked Questions is a project that could only be initiated by an individual who has a deep and involved experience with a social issue. The 'instinct' or 'nose' for a social problem isn't innate, it is often held by people who have been through homelessness. This is illustrated time and time again in the modern history of homelessness in the UK. In this history, individuals, often touched by the issues themselves, have taken action and started groups, movements or initiatives that simultaneously resist and create. It is something we see here with Gerald Mclaverty. Gerald's drive, borne out of his direct insight into - and frustration with - systems of care, led to the collaboration with Anthony, whose experience and artistic practice has enabled the co-development of a body of work.

Frequently Asked Questions works because of this pooling of these different skills and experiences. It is effective because it comes from that place of direct experience and its visually arresting presentation works to pique curiosity. You immediately want to

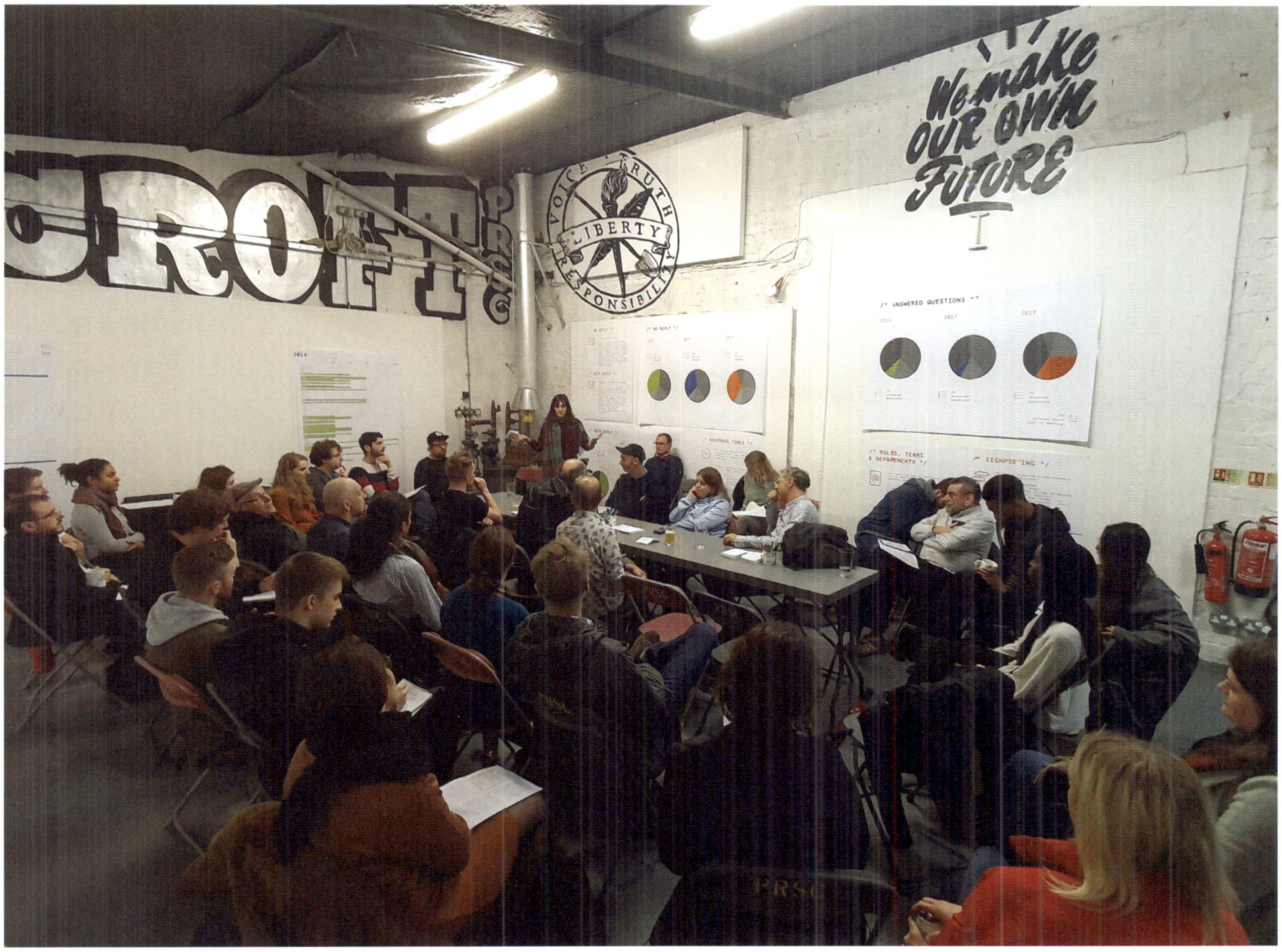


Rough State long table discussion with The Bristol Cable, Frequently Asked Questions, People's Republic of Stokes Croft, Bristol, 28th November 2019. Photograph by Lucas Batt

know how your council responded, and you want to know how the situation has changed over time. The viewer of Frequently Asked Questions is able to get their answers immediately, ironically. There is a personal connection fostered by seeing how your own local authority performs; a starting point for the discussion that so often follows in the gallery. Yet it is not just the head, but also the heart that is stimulated. Reading copies of the correspondence is illuminating and distressing in equal measure.

Why is it so hard for society to do something so simple as answer these questions? There are some immediate answers – swathing cuts to local authorities being the most obvious (the Local Government Association reports a £15.7 billion funding gap for English councils by 2020). But other, more historic, forces are at play too. Today's situation has its roots in the landmark 1977 Housing (Homeless Persons) Act, which made local authorities responsible for the long-term housing of some people in society for the first time. This piece of legislation has shaped the way that homelessness has been dealt with over the last 40 years, establishing a system of assessments, procedures, and prioritisation. Frequently Asked Questions shows us how strikingly the experience of homelessness can come into conflict with the legal and social structures designed around it.

Today's situation can also be traced to the historic emergence of a grassroots 'scene of care' in the 50s and 60s that evolved into a landscape of charitable enterprise, anchored around procurement contracts, databases, and professionalisation. These are the charities that now provide the majority of homelessness services. They are large and complex organisations and competitive tendering, combined with funding cuts, can mean 'a race to the bottom' with fewer and fewer resources for people in need. No wonder that the immediate answers can be hard to find.

In setting up the Museum of Homelessness (MoH) in 2015 we sought to create a hybrid social justice organisation/museum that could respond to injustice, stigma, and inequality. In working with Anthony and Gerald, we have found two people who share our ethos and commitment to social change through the arts. MoH has been uniquely privileged to be able to be part of the journey of Frequently Asked Questions. We've met regularly with Anthony and Gerald to discuss findings and share aspects of the museum's work that might inform the development of the project. We know that change often happens slowly, and a goal for MoH has been to bring together people to unpack the complexities of the homelessness crisis.

Frequently Asked Questions tangibly demonstrates that if you look beyond simplistic media headlines and government soundbites, the real picture of how things work on the ground is grossly unsatisfactory and illogical.

Perhaps due to deepening inequalities and political turmoil in the UK, many cultural institutions are now seeking to carry out work that is 'activist' in nature or 'socially engaged'. Anthony's artistic practice has always had this at its core and this is what makes Frequently Asked Questions such a potent and authentic body of work, at a time when these questions are more important than ever.

Jess and Matt Turtle
Co-founders, Museum of Homelessness

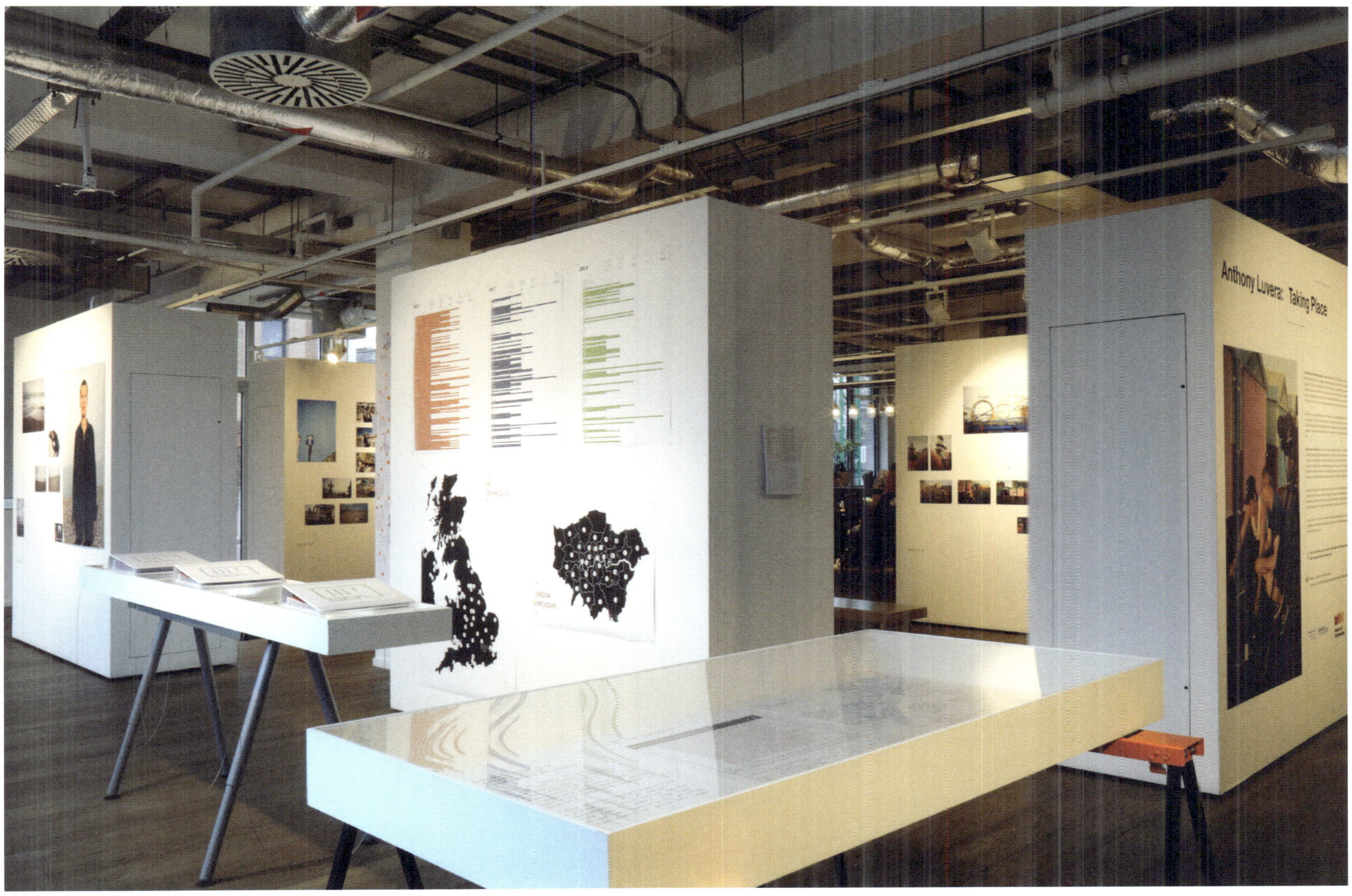


Frequently Asked Questions, Anthony Luvera: Taking Place,
The Gallery at Foyles, London, 11th January to 29th February 2020

**Frequently Asked Questions**
Anthony Luvera
Gerald Mclaverty

With special thanks to:
Will Brady
Kate Elliott
Adam Hemmings
François Matarasso
Gerald Mclaverty
Tom Pye
Brighton Photo Fringe
Rebecca Drew
Laura Mousavi
Jane Noble
Brighton Housing Trust
Tracey Chandler
Marek Coskry
Simon Hughes
The Bristol Cable
Lucas Batt
Cait Crosse
Coventry University
Rosamund Buxton
Andrea Crowley
Neil Forbes
Louise Moody
Futurecity
Mark Davy
Sherry Dobbin
Elen Salina
Chloe Stagaman
IC Visual Lab
Alejandro Acin
Liverpool Salon
Pauline Hadaway
Museum of Homelessness
Jess Turtle
Matt Turtle
People's Republic of Stokes Croft
Benoit Bennett
Chris Chalkley
Tony Fortune
Lisa Furness
Tate Liverpool
Michael Birchall
Jessica Fairclough
Lindsey Fryer

Design by Will Brady
Published by Dulwich Road Studio Press
ISBN: 978-1-9163733-0-3

Paper supplied by G . F Smith.
Text: Munken Design Lynx Smooth 150gsm
Cover: Munken Design Lynx Smooth 240gsm



Museum of Homelessness

Research Centre Arts, Memory and Communities | Coventry University

**About Anthony Luvera**
Anthony is an Australian artist, writer, and educator based in London. For over 15 years he has worked with people who have experienced homelessness in cities and towns across the United Kingdom, including Belfast, Brighton, Colchester, and in various boroughs across London. This has led to the creation of a collection of thousands of photographs created by participants, the on-going series Assisted Self-Portraits, and other works using photography, video, sound recording, performance, participative research, and public discussion events. His work has been exhibited widely in galleries, public spaces, and festivals, including the British Museum, London Underground's Art on the Underground, National Portrait Gallery London, Belfast Exposed Photography, Australian Centre for Photography, PhotoIreland, Malmö Fotobiennal, Goa International Photography Festival, and Les Rencontres D'ArlesPhotographie. His writing appears regularly in a wide range of publications including Photoworks, Source, and Photographies. Anthony is Associate Professor of Photography in the Centre for Arts, Memory and Communities at Coventry University, and editor of Photography For Whom?, a periodical about socially engaged photography. He also designs education and mentorship programmes, facilitates workshops, and gives lectures for the public education departments of Tate Britain, the National Portrait Gallery, Royal Academy of Arts, The Photographers' Gallery, Photofusion, Barbican Art Gallery, Magnum Photos, and community photography projects across the UK.
www.luvera.com

**About Museum of Homelessness**
The Museum of Homelessness (MoH) is the first of its kind in the UK and has been created by people with direct experience of homelessness. Our community explores the art, history, and culture of homelessness to make a difference for people experiencing homelessness today. We make the invisible visible through collecting, research, events, and exhibitions.
www.museumofhomelessness.org

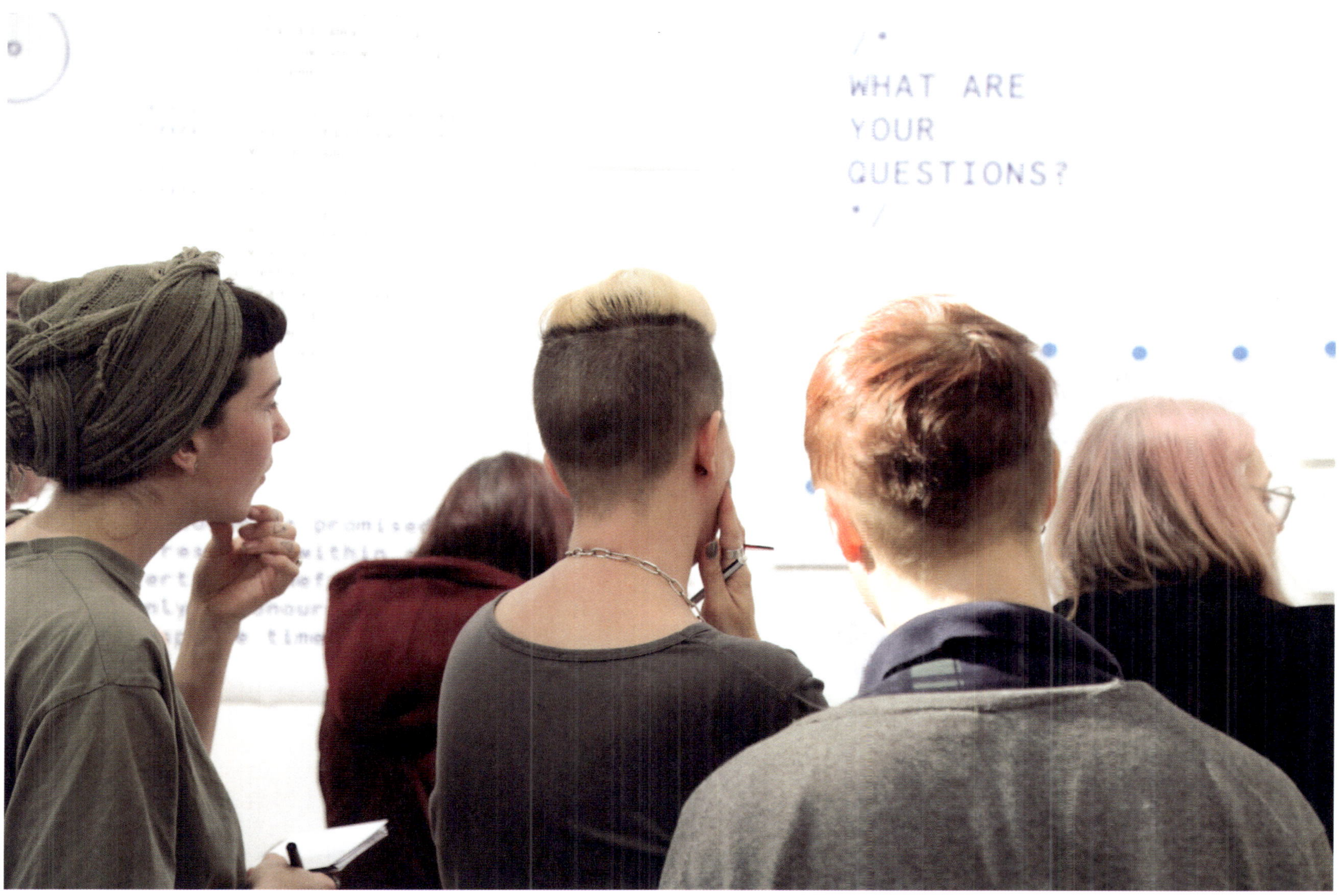


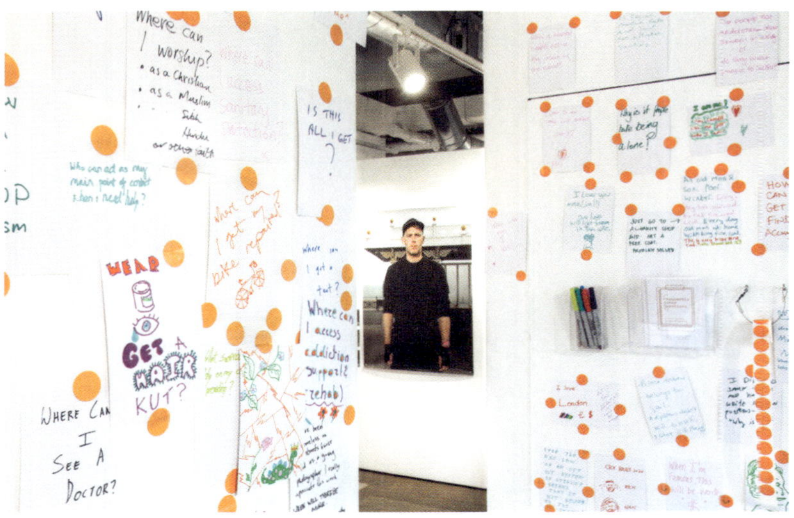


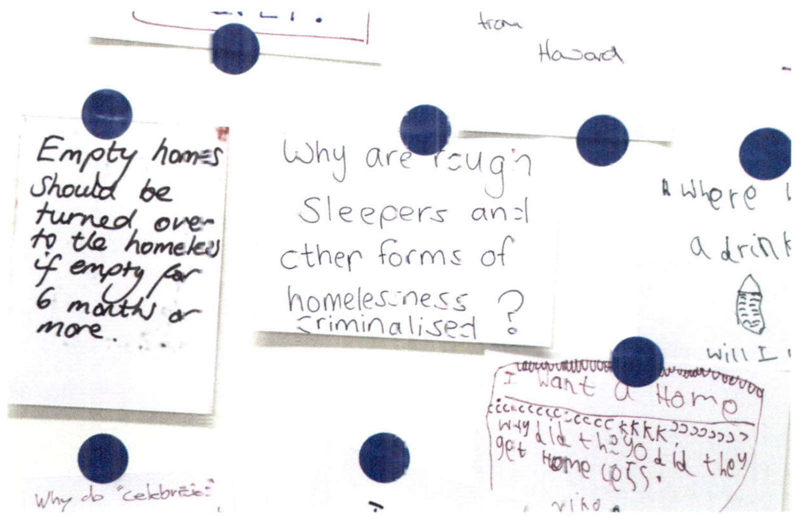


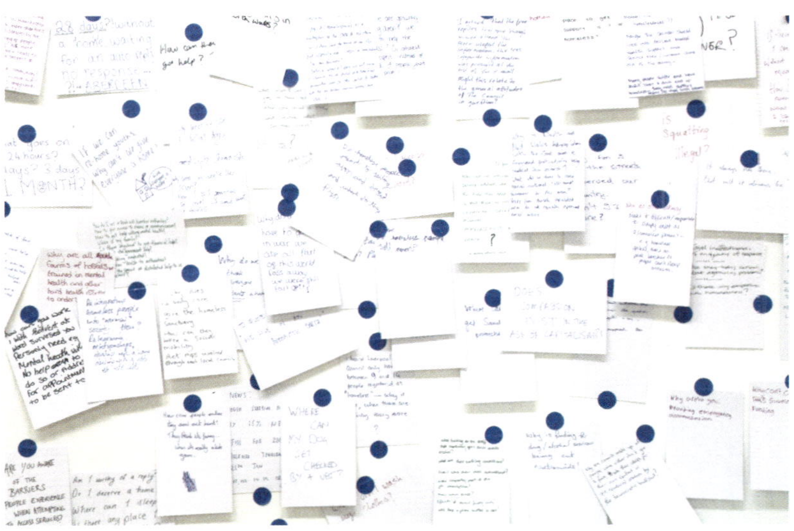

What are your questions?, Frequently Asked Questions, Tate Liverpool (2018), People's Republic of Stokes Croft, Bristol (2019), The Gallery at Foyles, London (2020)

9 781916 373303